# Holy Angels

## Marc Thomas

First published by Dog Ear Publishing
4011 Vincennes Rd
Indianapolis, IN 46268
www.dogearpublishing.net

ISBN: 978-1-4575-5889-4

This book is printed on acid-free paper.

This book is a work of fiction. Places, events, and situations in this book are purely fic-
tional and any resemblance to actual persons, living or dead, is coincidental.

Printed in the United States of America

# Holy Angels

# CHAPTER

# 1

## Late April

"Dammit!"

The figure on the sofa jerked his head up reflexively at the realization he had overslept. Brushing gray hair out of his eyes, he squinted at the clock on the wall. "Nine-thirty! I gotta pick Ellen up at the airport at eleven, and it's an hour's drive!"

Robert Wexford stood up but had to prop himself against the sofa to keep from falling. He was extremely hung over, his head was about to explode and his bladder was bursting. *You idiot, why didn't you go to sleep earlier? And you had to go and drain the entire bottle of wine? This isn't college anymore.*

He looked down at the open Styrofoam container on the coffee table. A few bites of barbeque from Famous Willie's remained, and he suddenly realized he was hungry, but the leftovers didn't appeal to him. He'd grab something on the way to the airport, or maybe after picking his wife up. Not enough time to worry about it now. He had fallen asleep watching the NFL Draft on television the night before, after making the ten hour trek by car from Seattle to their vacation home on Lake Coeur d'Alene, Idaho.

He splashed cold water on his face and slapped a brush through his hair, gargled a bit and threw on some clothes.

Robert rubbed his eyes again as he maneuvered the SUV out of the driveway and through the addition. Barring a traffic jam in Spokane, he figured he'd arrive just about the time Ellen was landing.

As he made his way onto I-90 north of town and headed west toward the airport, the hangover started to recede, helped along by a couple of diet sodas and an aspirin. He almost fell asleep again on the outskirts of Spokane, lulled into a trance by the repeating scenes of tall pines and rolling farmland, but managed to perk up when he passed the sign for Gonzaga University. It reminded him of his own alma mater, Holy Cross College in Massachusetts, another Jesuit school. A few minutes later he pulled into short-term parking at the airport and headed for the terminal.

Once inside, he glanced at the flight schedule and noted that Ellen's plane had landed five minutes before. *She's probably down in baggage claim. I'll run down there,* he thought. But when he arrived, there was no sign of his wife. A few pieces of luggage moved slowly around the conveyor belt, but none looked familiar. Robert asked a bystander if the passengers had come and gone, and she nodded affirmatively. He then tried calling Ellen on his phone, but it went to voicemail. Puzzled, he wandered out the exit and looked around. There, to his far left, was Ellen, talking to someone on her cell phone and gesticulating.

"Ellen!!"

The volume and irritated tone of Robert's shout startled not only her, but also others who were standing around waiting to be picked up. She pressed the phone to her chest and frowned. "It's Lynda! I saw your number come through, but you know how she is. Give me a break, Rob. She called as soon as I got off the plane."

He glared at her. "I've been trying to find you for a good fifteen minutes, Ellen. Think about it. Are we gonna resume what we left unfinished in Seattle? I don't want that. It's our vacation, come on. Tell her you'll call her back later, let's get out of here."

Robert was irritated. They had had a disagreement two days before at their home on Mercer Island outside Seattle, and it hadn't gotten resolved. The disputes were becoming more frequent, and the anxiety level for both of them had shot up as a result. Still, he wanted this week's get-away to work for both of them, so he pushed his anger aside and tried to smooth things over.

"Well, OK, I'll pull the truck around and meantime, you try to end the call."

Ellen clutched the phone, looked at him with resignation and slowly pulled her suitcases over to the curb as her husband walked away.

No more than five minutes had elapsed on the ride back to Coeur d'Alene before Robert suddenly realized he needed to get something in his stomach. He was hungry but at the same time, also weirdly nauseated from all the wine he had consumed, and he was guessing that food would solve both problems. "Listen, Ellen, I've gotta have something to eat. You hungry? I can stop at this next exit, there's a convenience store there."

She nodded yes. Five minutes later, Robert was standing in a line at the store counter, waiting to pay for the sandwiches and drinks he cradled in his arms. Ellen was waiting for him at the door, looking at magazines.

An old woman was fishing through her purse at the counter, the store clerk standing with his hand out, waiting for payment. "I know I have the correct change in here somewhere," she pleaded.

Just then, Robert stuck his head out of the line and shouted, "Come on, ma'am. Some of us are in a hurry. We haven't got all day!"

Those around him turned and nervously shuffled their feet. It was obvious they weren't as upset or in a hurry as Robert was. The shouted remark made the woman even more flustered. Suddenly, Robert stepped out of line and strode toward the counter, a ten-dollar bill hanging from his fingers. He dropped it in the cashier's hand and gestured toward the woman. "That's for hers and mine. We've gotta get out of here." He stepped toward the door and motioned for Ellen to follow. With a look of embarrassment, she held the door for him and they walked to their truck.

"Why did you make such a big scene, Rob? We're not in that much of a hurry. We're not going anywhere once we get to the house."

"Yeah, yeah, I know. I just wanted to get out of there. Hungry, you know. And tired. I didn't sleep well last night, probably my fault. After I got into town I worked out, got a bottle at the liquor store, went out to Post Falls for barbeque take-out, then crashed at the house watching the draft. Had to see who the Bills picked - of course they take a quarterback who couldn't hit the ocean from the beach. Then drank too much wine. I'm pissed off in general."

Ellen looked out the window as she took another bite from her sandwich. For her, the story was depressingly familiar. She was married to a successful physical therapist, but the reasons for his success were the same ones now impacting their relationship in a negative way – impatience, an outsized opinion of self and impossible expectations placed on those around him. It was never good enough for Robert and she was growing tired of bearing the brunt of it.

"You shouldn't have done that to that old woman at the counter. Just relax. It'll go a long way for you, and for us."

He glanced at her and took a long swig of his drink. He was too tired to argue.

"And, oh, by the way, I've got this here for you. It came in the mail yesterday." She pulled an envelope from her purse and held it out for him.

"Can't you read it to me?" he said. "I've got a drink in one hand, a sandwich between my legs and the other hand on the steering wheel."

"I won't tell you who it's from, you'll know as soon as I start reading it."

"OK, shoot," he said.

"As many of you are aware, the board of directors of your alma mater, Holy Angels Academy, has spent the past few months discussing ways to ensure that the doors of this proud institution stay open. In short, the school needs to raise $400,000 by July 1st in order to continue operations for the coming school year. Reaching this goal will necessitate the continued generosity of alumni and benefactors, people such as yourself….."

"Enough already!" Robert bellowed, with a look of disgust. "What is the matter with that place? Every couple of years, they ask for money. Every couple of years, they dream up some 'plan' that's gonna fix the school's finances once and for all. Then they get the money and bingo, a year or two later they're on death's door again. This is no way to run a high school! Trust me, I know from my own upbringing where we were one step ahead of the creditors all the time. Get someone in there who knows what they're doing."

Ellen put the letter down and calmly asked, "So, does that mean there's no help forthcoming from the Wexfords?"

"Damn right it does," he thundered. His grip on the steering wheel was tightening.

"We've sent money a number of times before. It's being pissed down the toilet. Hey, it's not my problem anymore. If Westport doesn't want a Catholic high school, then the people will answer with their wallets and feet. Let someone else carry their water for a change."

Robert eventually calmed down and the couple arrived back at the house an hour later. After unpacking their bags, they opened a bottle of wine and headed for the deck out back overlooking the lake. On the way there, Robert noticed the envelope from his high school in upstate New York still hanging out of his wife's purse. He took another cursory look at the letter, wadded it up and tossed it unceremoniously in the trashcan under the kitchen sink.

The next few days of their vacation were spent doing the things both of them enjoyed while in Coeur d'Alene. Ellen spent afternoons perusing the downtown shops on the lookout for Indian jewelry and antiques, Robert took long walks along the lake's perimeter, and both of them did some biking. Evenings found them at one of the various small local eateries they favored.

Their personal disagreements had been put on the back burner.

# CHAPTER

## 2

The following Friday, Robert was half-asleep on the lower-level when he heard his cell phone ringing. He leaped off the couch, bounded up the stairs, and grabbed the phone just before it went to voicemail.

"Hello." He immediately recognized the voice on the other end. "Tom?" Robert asked. "Tom, how are you?"

"Hey, Rob. How's it going?"

Tom Sarrazin was an old friend of Robert's from his time in Indianapolis, before Robert and Ellen moved out West to be closer to her family. Tom was also a physical therapist who practiced in a competing group. Tom's wife Nancy and Ellen Wexford were close, and the couples had maintained a relationship despite their current geographical separation.

After a couple minutes of small talk, Tom said, "Rob, you haven't heard about Alex, have you?"

Robert frowned. Alex was a mutual friend of theirs, a very successful Indianapolis businessman and someone they both held in high esteem. His voice lowered. "No, what's up?"

Tom said, "Well, he hadn't been feeling well for a few months, so he went to the doctor and they ran some tests. Turns out they found a large tumor in his liver. They biopsied it, and it came back malignant - liver cancer."

Robert blanched. He knew that liver cancer was almost uniformly fatal, especially if it was diagnosed late. He held the phone to his ear as his hand slightly trembled.

Tom said, "Well, they couldn't operate because it was wrapped around his vena cava. So they sent him to Pittsburgh to see if he was eligible for a liver transplant. The guy there said no way, because of the vena cava being involved, and also because of his weight and with the bad heart. So they told him to see someone at Northwestern in Chicago who has had some success freezing tumors – you know, cryotherapy. Now, all of the time this is going on, he's got his entire parish praying for him, and the parish priest, who's Indian, has his seminary back home praying for him, 600 strong."

Robert smiled. "And don't forget, Alex's uncle was the archbishop of Indianapolis back in the '50s."

"Right," Tom said. "So the Chicago guy wants a new set of CT scans of the liver before he does anything to Alex, because it's been a few weeks since his last one. Alex goes up there and has them done, then he's driving back home on I-65 when his phone rings. He pulls over and takes the call. The doc is all excited – the radiologists went over the scans with him and there was no sign of any tumor."

Robert reached for a nearby chair and steadied himself as he sat.

Tom's voice quivered. "So, Alex tells me that God has done something wonderful for him, that this meant that God had some purpose for him in life. He ends up donating $2 million to build an education center for the parish."

Robert stared blankly ahead. His mind was like a boxing ring at the moment, with competing explanations for what he'd been told battling like two heavyweights trading haymakers in the center. Which one would prevail – the empirical, rational side that had been instilled in him by the Jesuits at Holy Cross, and which had come to dominate his thinking ever since? Or the belief system he had developed during his years as a traditional Catholic, the one that left room for miracles to explain the unexplainable? It didn't take him long to come down on the side of the former, but he kept his deliberations to himself as Tom finished the story. Robert asked Tom to convey his best wishes to Alex and his family, and after a few more minutes of small talk, he hung up the phone.

He sat motionless in the chair and looked out the huge kitchen window at Lake Coeur d'Alene for what seemed an eternity. *This couldn't be anything more than a coincidence,* he thought. *Case reports exist of tumors that vanish without apparent explanation. But if I'm going all rational on this, then what is the rational explanation? Maybe science isn't advanced enough to tell us now. It'll be obvious down the road, when we know more. Of course!*

He felt a little more comfortable.

His eyes turned from the lake and darted from object to object in the kitchen. On the counter was a small plastic bottle of water with blue etching on its face. The sight jarred his memory. The bottle was one of two that had been given to the Wexfords by a friend who'd made a pilgrimage to the Catholic shrine at Lourdes, France.

Robert learned the story of Lourdes during his grade school days. In February of 1858, an illiterate peasant girl, Bernadette Soubirous, reported that a series of apparitions appeared in a rocky niche on a riverbank. The woman in the apparition told her to dig in the soil along the bank. The girl did so and a spring welled up. Numerous reports were documented of people with various illnesses cured of their afflictions after bathing in the spring. Bernadette was eventually canonized, and her unembalmed yet uncorrupted body still lies in a glass coffin in a convent in central France. Robert was reminded this was yet another phenomenon without any rational explanation.

*Wait a minute!*

He thought of another phone call he'd received a few months before, in late January. College friend Chris Talieres had asked Robert to pray for his one-year-old grandson who had been born with a bad heart. A ventricular assist device was implanted to help the boy's heart contract but it was only a temporary measure. The child needed a heart transplant. On the phone call, Chris was under the assumption that his friend was still the church-going Catholic he knew at Holy Cross.

Robert wasn't that guy anymore, but he sympathized with his friend's plight and offered one of the Lourdes bottles, instructing Chris to have the water sprinkled over the child on occasion. He knew that Chris was a practicing Orthodox Christian and would follow through. But now, three months had elapsed and Robert had forgotten about the whole episode. He felt a sudden urge to find out what had happened to the little boy.

He picked up his cell phone, fished Chris' number out of the contact list and left a voice message. About 20 minutes later, the phone rang.

"Jack!" said the voice on the other end. Robert knew it had to be Chris. Only his college buddies referred to him by that name, and he was ready with his friend's nickname as well.

"Greek!"

"How the hell are you, Jack? Hey, I was meaning to call you and let you know what happened to Alex."

Robert's eyebrows raised as he was reminded by his friend of the little boy's name. *Alex, and now another Alex! Two people with the same name, two life-changing events, and I find out about them a few minutes apart? What the hell is going on here?*

He was hanging on every one of The Greek's words.

"Yeah, Jack. You're not going to believe what I'm gonna tell you. We talked in late January, I believe. A few weeks later, the transplant team called in the middle of the night, told my son and daughter-in-law to pack their bags and drive like hell to Birmingham. They had a heart ready and they did the transplant in the morning. He's about eight weeks out now and doing well. He's got a great appetite and is gaining weight!"

Robert felt like he was spitting cotton. "Greek, this is wonderful! I…uh…we're so happy for you and your family."

Eventually, the conversation turned to other topics, like where their old college buddies should have their annual get-together. But Robert wasn't going to hang up until he knew what had happened to the bottle of water he'd sent. "Greek, tell me something. That Lourdes bottle I gave you…"

"I know, I know. I can't believe I didn't mention that. My son and daughter-in-law did just as you said with it. I can't help but believe that it worked."

Robert's voice sharpened. "Greek, listen. I need to know when the transplant happened."

"Uh, well, it was a couple or three weeks after we talked."

"I need the exact date."

"Wow, you sound serious all of a sudden. He got the transplant on February 12th."

Robert stiffened up. "They got the call in the middle of the night on the 12th? Does that mean that the donor heart became available a few hours before that?"

"Well, yes. But what's the significance?"

Robert bounded down the stairs to his laptop. He fumbled opening it and asked his friend to stay on the line while he powered it up. Two minutes later, he was typing furiously into the Google query box.

"Hold on Greek, just a minute. Oh boy. Oh boy."

"Jack, what's the deal? You're killing me, my friend!"

Robert took a deep breath. "February 11th is the feast day of Our Lady of Lourdes. That's the date of the first apparition. Your grandson's new heart became available on the feast day of Our Lady of Lourdes."

# CHAPTER

## 3

The next morning Ellen peered into her coffee cup for what seemed like an eternity. It felt like such a waste to spend the last Saturday of their Coeur d'Alene vacation sitting at home. She had suggested heading into town before the stores opened at 10, where she could do a little shopping while Robert wandered around absent-mindedly with his trademark cup of green tea, but he was noncommittal. *Something's up,* she thought. *He seems preoccupied.*

She ran her hand through her long auburn hair and decided to find out what was bothering him. Ellen walked over to the large coffee table in front of the sofa, sat down on the corner and faced her husband. "Rob, something going on? Here we are on vaca in your favorite place. It's fantastic outside, and you don't want to move. Please tell me what's going on inside that head."

He responded slowly, in monotone, without looking at her. "I don't know. Something happened yesterday. I didn't tell you about it last night because...well, I didn't know how to put it, whether or not it was important. But I might as well tell you now that you ask."

He pivoted and stared into her eyes. "Tom Sarrazin called yesterday, before you got back from town. He told me something about Alex from Indianapolis. Alex was diagnosed with a large tumor in his liver. Couldn't be operated on. People prayed for him. A few weeks later, he went to Chicago to see if the tumor could be 'frozen' by some specialist. He got another CT scan, before the procedure. It showed that the tumor had disappeared. On its own, with no treatment whatsoever."

11

Ellen leaned back, and her eyes widened. "That's wonderful. I mean unbelievable, but wonderful. So happy for him and Judy and the family." She paused, arching her eyebrows. "So what do you think caused that?"

She had a feeling her husband knew where she was going with the question. She was testing him, attempting to get him to commit to one of only two possible conclusions anyone could draw about what happened to their friend.

He continued, "I'm not finished yet. A few minutes later, I saw that Lourdes water bottle on the kitchen counter. You remember, I sent the other one to Chris Talieres for the grandson who needed the heart transplant."

Ellen nodded.

"I decided to call him to find out what happened to the kid. It turns out that he did get a new heart, had the operation about three weeks after I sent the bottle. The donor heart became available on the feast day of Lourdes, February 11th."

Ellen was silent. For a few seconds they stared at each other, expressionless. Robert finally broke the silence.

"I know what you're thinking. You think I believe it's all a coincidence, that there must be some scientific or medical explanation for both stories. Look, the heart becoming available happened when it happened. It may well be a coincidence it was that day. I can buy that. But adult Alex? I don't know, harder to explain that one. And here's the other odd thing. The Talieres kid's name is…"

She widened her eyes. "Don't tell me it's Alex!"

He smiled. "Yup. So, if you are wondering why I'm slowly wasting this great day, that's why. Just bothered by it all."

Robert loved bragging to people he was Catholic. But he didn't have much use for the actual practice of it. Maybe it was all that Jesuit education at Holy Cross, where they basically peeled away the faith of your youth and dared you to replace it, either with a more mature version having its justification in intellectual rigor or with something else. Unfortunately for many of their students, the "something else" too often turned out to be "nothing". And like it or not, that's how the Jesuits operate.

Robert attended Mass on occasion, but it was more going through the motions, done so that others would buy the ruse that he was still a believer. The charade and self- deception extended to other aspects of his life, as well. He was involved in social endeavors but not out of a sense of civic duty. He did it so that the hosannas that came with volunteering piled high upon his considerable ego. It was all about Robert, and no one was more aware of it than, well, Robert.

But yesterday's events had him thinking. Maybe it was time to head to church, if only to sit there and wait for an answer he really didn't expect to get. *You never know,* he thought.

He ran his fingers through his hair and said, "Ellen, I think we need to go to Mass tomorrow."

# CHAPTER

## 4

Robert yawned as he maneuvered the SUV into the parking lot at St. Matthew's Church in Post Falls. On the occasions when the Wexfords attended Mass, they usually went west of town to this small enclave, home to a traditional Catholic church where the Latin Mass was celebrated.

Ellen didn't much care for it. For the most part the liturgy was devoid of singing, and the congregation was left to follow along using their Latin "cheat sheets" while the priest and altar servers turned their backs to them and mumbled unintelligibly in the ancient official tongue of the Church.

Robert on the other hand much preferred it. This was what he had grown up with prior to Vatican II, the 1960s council that modernized the Mass. He had little use for the current ceremony, with its emphasis on audience participation and a hefty dose of music. He turned to his wife and smiled. "At least we won't have a hootenanny. I really couldn't take it this early in the morning. And besides, you won't have to hear my off-key singing too much."

Ellen shook her head and opened the car door. "I'm doing this for you. I would have preferred going into town where they have a regular Mass."

He smiled. "I have a better chance of getting an answer here. God only speaks in Latin, you know."

The couple walked in after the service started and took their place in a back pew, just before the first reading. Robert's mind was already wandering, but he did catch that the passage was from the First Book of Kings. It began with the prophet Elijah being pursued by his enemies and fleeing into the desert. Robert's eyes widened and he listened intently to this part:

"There, he came to a cave, where he took shelter. But the word of the Lord came to him, "Why are you here, Elijah? Then the Lord said, 'Go outside and stand on the mountain before the Lord; the Lord will be passing by.' A strong and heavy wind was rending the mountains and crushing rocks before the Lord – but the Lord was not in the wind. After the wind there was an earthquake – but the Lord was not in the earthquake. After the earthquake there was fire – but the Lord was not in the fire. After the fire, there was a tiny whispering sound."

Robert fixated on the last few words. He'd gotten little sleep the night before thinking of the two unexplained "miracles" that his friends had experienced. He shifted in the pew and wondered. *Is somebody trying to tell me something? Could the two happenings be my 'tiny whispering sound?'*

After Mass, the crowd filed slowly out the front entrance to the church, its progress slowed as people paused to chat with the celebrant, Father Miles. Robert held his hand up to Ellen as they stood in the entranceway. He waited until most of the crowd left, then made his way over to the priest. The white-haired man gave him a look of vague recognition and extended a hand.

"Hello, Father. Robert and Ellen Wexford. How are you?"

"Fine, fine. Good to see you two."

"Hey, Father. If you have a minute, I'd like to tell you something. And I also have a question."

The priest nodded, jowls bobbing up and down. Robert decided to begin with an untruth. "Really enjoyed your homily today, Father." The reality was that he fell asleep halfway through the Mass. He then quickly changed the subject to avoid discussing the sermon. "Something weird happened to me Friday, Father. Maybe you can help." He described the events of two days ago, taking care to stress the odd similarity and timing between the stories of his friend Alex and his friend's grandson, Alex.

Father Miles listened intently, his eyes narrowing as Robert spoke.

"I guess I'm not sure what to make of all this, Father. Do you think God's trying to tell me something, or is it coincidence? One minute I find out one friend is cured of an incurable cancer. And then, it's kind of strange that the little boy's heart became available on the feast of Lourdes, three weeks after I gave his grandfather the bottle of Lourdes spring water."

The old priest put his hands on his ample midsection and laughed. "You know the definition of coincidence, don't you?"

Ellen and Robert shrugged.

"Coincidence is God's way of saying, 'I'm still around.' "

# CHAPTER

## 5

The rolling farmland of northwest Idaho served as an excuse for Ellen to stare vacantly out the window of the SUV as they returned from church to their vacation home. Her husband hadn't spoken since they left the parking lot in Post Falls 15 minutes ago. She decided to break the ice.

"What are you thinking, Rob?"

He kept his gaze straight ahead on the road and cleared his throat. "Still wondering what it all means. I'm beginning to think it happened this way for a reason, and I'm trying to figure out what it means for me."

Ellen stared at the dashboard for a few seconds. "It might be nice to figure it out soon. Because if it's more than chance these things happened the way they did, perhaps the answer to your question sits right in front of you, and you don't see it."

Her husband looked furtively at her, extended his hands on the steering wheel, and angled his head back onto the seat. Then, out of the blue, a thought hit him. Without saying a word, he pressed a little harder on the gas pedal to hasten their arrival.

After they got back he didn't wait for his wife to exit the vehicle, instead he bounded up the front stairs and hurriedly unlocked the door. When Ellen finally caught up to him in the kitchen, he was rummaging through the trashcan under the sink, tossing items on the floor and cursing under his breath.

"What in God's name are you looking for?" she asked.

A few seconds later, his hand emerged from the container. Red tomato sauce and fragments of a banana slice dripped onto the floor as he held up a crumpled paper. Robert placed the paper on the countertop and carefully wiped the sticky debris off as best he could. "This is my 'whispering sound,' Ellen. This is what I need to do."

The crumpled paper was the Holy Angels letter he'd tossed away a few days before.

In an excited tone, he said, "I'm going to help my old school stay open. I'm gonna do something to make sure they don't close."

Ellen looked at him suspiciously. She knew Robert, knew what kind of person he was, especially when an opportunity cropped up to wear his "generosity" like a badge. *Hmm, shades of the time he donated all that money to the Hope Center in Seattle. Turns out he did it after he found out the major benefactors were invited to a televised ribbon cutting. Now his hometown school is looking for a hero. Could this be instant replay?*

"How are you going to help them, Rob? Maybe throw them a donation? That would make you look good."

He slowly shook his head and smiled, half embarrassed and more than a trifle offended by her insinuation. "You know, a guy can't have one good idea without someone tossing cynical remarks around. Maybe, just maybe I really want to help out, and I'm not talking about a donation. Maybe I want to go back there myself and help them raise money. How about that?" His indignation was escalating rapidly.

Ellen's green eyes flashed. "Look, I'm your wife. I've known you for 30-some years, know how you think, how you operate. OK, maybe you do have good intentions this time, but could there be an eentsy-weentsy bit of self-aggrandizement going on as well? You go back there, help them out, give them a hefty donation to boot, and you're gonna look good to your hometown regardless of whether Holy Angels stays open or not. They'll be talking for years to come about how the guy from the West Coast rode in and single-handedly tried to keep his high school's doors open. You'll come out smelling like a rose regard..."

She didn't have a chance to finish. Robert tossed the soaking-wet letter in her direction and stormed out of the room. No question Ellen had touched a nerve, but her husband's true intentions were still unclear to her.

After regaining his composure in the study, he admitted to himself that he had, in the past, been a little selfish whenever he did something purportedly good. But he was becoming convinced this time would be different. The priest's words hit home hard in a way he'd never felt before. This was no series of coincidences, and he had to do *something* about it, just like his friend Alex had done by donating all that money to his church after his cancer disappeared.

And if things didn't pan out? *At least they'll know Robert Wexford tried.*

He pivoted and stared at his reflection in the mirror.

# CHAPTER

## 6

Robert was still upset about yesterday's exchange with Ellen. He flipped the radio on, interrupting the silence that filled the SUV on the way to take Ellen back to the airport. His wife, meanwhile, sat motionless in the passenger seat, eyes straight ahead and arms folded, a position she'd kept since they left the house. He knew she dreaded the lonely plane ride back to Seattle, not to mention what would almost certainly occur when her husband returned later that day after driving back – more of the silent treatment.

Robert pulled the SUV up to the airport departure curb, extracted Ellen's bags from the trunk, and kissed her on the forehead before saying goodbye. After her figure disappeared through the sliding glass doors, he climbed back into the cab and drove off.

Once back on the interstate, he fleetingly contemplated his dysfunctional marriage but quickly decided he preferred to dwell on something more positive. Thoughts turned to the more exciting and interesting prospect of going back to Westport to help save Holy Angels.

The first order of business was to obtain permission from his physical therapy partners for a leave of absence. He'd work on that as soon as he got back to Seattle. But he also suddenly realized how compressed the timeline was for raising all that money. It was already the first of May, and the deadline for the school to raise the $400,000 it needed to stay open was the first of July – a scant eight weeks away. It seemed an almost insurmountable task to come up with that much money in that short a span, especially considering the state of the economy in his hometown.

Westport fit the stereotype of the post-industrial blue-collar town, long on spirit but short on finances. Many residents had fled the state in search of jobs and lower taxes, moving south to places like the Carolinas and Florida. Not helping matters was the fact that demographics had changed dramatically over the years, with increasing numbers of seniors and fewer families with children. Robert surmised a smaller applicant pool was part of the school's problem, but also wondered how much the administrative missteps he had mentioned to Ellen had to do with it. Whatever, he had had a change of heart about it all, and he knew he wanted to go back now.

But he also was cognizant that he had only superficial knowledge of what was really going on with Holy Angels, snippets and fragments he had heard the past few years from friends back home. He needed to find out the real scoop, and to do that he had to talk to someone on the inside. It didn't take more than a few seconds for him to figure out who that was.

"Tilly DeAngelo! Yes!"

Theodore "Tilly" DeAngelo belonged to one of Westport's many generational Italian families. He was one class behind Robert at Holy Angels, and although the two of them knew each other only superficially in high school, they had become fast friends as part of a group that attended Notre Dame football games on a regular basis. Among others, that group included Dan Herlihy, the varsity football coach at Angels. Tilly knew everyone in Westport and Robert was almost positive he was on the Angels school board as well.

He pulled off the next exit and parked the truck at the nearest gas station. A quick flip through his contact list produced the number.

"Hey, Tilly. How's it goin'? Rob Wexford here!"

"Rob, how the hell are you? Haven't heard from you in a while, since that BC game in South Bend a couple of years ago. You going this fall with us? Or have you finally wised up?"

Robert laughed. "No, I'm still dumb as hell and itching for more punishment. But this next time, I stop at three beers!" They both laughed. "Seriously, I'm calling about Holy Angels and this fund drive they're having. Are you still on the board at the school? I thought I saw your name on the letterhead."

"Unfortunately, yes. And I'm only partly kidding when I say that," said Tilly. "I thought being on city council was tough – you ought to be on the board of a failing Catholic high school, with everyone blaming everyone else for the situation they've gotten themselves into. You know, this should be the time when a board is of one mind and purpose, and it ain't happening. We need working groups and a well-thought-out plan, neither of which we have. You wanna take my place?"

Tilly proceeded to emit one of his patented belly-laughs.

This wasn't what Robert wanted to hear. It would be difficult enough raising that kind of money in two months, but near impossible without consensus on how to do it. It sounded like they were floundering. A knot formed in his stomach, and he realized his grand vision was already coming apart at the seams.

"Hey, Rob! You still there?"

"Uh, yeah. Just listening. Sounds bad. You think it can be salvaged?"

Tilly said, "Right now, no. Too many cooks in the kitchen having more fun throwing food at each other instead of making the meal. No one's in charge, it seems. How about someone with gravitas coming in and taking the bull by the horns?"

Robert happily pounced on this remark. "Whoa, 'gravitas!' Another big word you learned in Catholic school, DeAngelo?"

Both of them laughed again.

"Tilly, you know what gravitas means, don't you? It means someone with the balls to pull this thing off. Or maybe someone stupid enough to try."

"Yeah, Rob. Someone with the gonads to get in here and get it done. We still have time but it's getting short." He paused and then asked, "Hey, why don't *you* help us out?"

A few seconds of silence elapsed.

"Hey, Wexford. Wake up! Bad connection?"

Robert stared out the truck window. "I'm awake, Tilly. Just thinking. Hey, thanks for the info. I may be calling you back soon. Bye!"

No sooner was Robert back on the interstate than he began day-dreaming. He started thinking about his journey through life and realized that Westport wasn't where the journey started. He had actually been born and raised in Columbia, a small town in the Southern Tier, the name given to the far southwestern corner of upstate New York. He thought back to the distant past, to the days of his childhood.

# CHAPTER

## 7

### *August 1960*

The young boy glanced furtively behind him at the rear corner of the neighbor's house. He saw no one from his vantage point next to the small pine tree at the front corner of the house. Still, he crouched silently, straining to pick up any sound that would indicate one of his "tag" partners was in the vicinity. There was no sound except for the distant occasional low rumble of a car engine. After a few minutes his attention lapsed, and he was startled by a rustling sound behind him.

"You're it!" a small voice exclaimed triumphantly. Freddie ran up and fell to his knees beside Robert Wexford. The intruder giggled uncontrollably, his belly quivering beneath the too-small T-shirt he was sporting.

Initially crestfallen at his discovery, Robert quickly disposed of the thought and rolled over in the lush green grass, joining his best friend in laughter. He glanced at Freddie and thought how wonderful life was this summer - days filled with endless games of tag, football, and baseball, the birthday parties, marshmallow roasts on the hillside at the end of the street, even a neighborhood circus organized by Freddie's parents.

His contentment abruptly ended as a sudden, more basic urge overtook him. "I have to pee," he announced. "Go on and look for everyone else."

Freddie nodded and ran off. Robert brushed his pants, straightened his denim jacket, and ran through neighbors' yards toward home to take care of business. When he arrived he noticed a pickup truck parked in the street next to the side porch. Several items of furniture were in the truck, and he realized they belonged to his family. Puzzled, Robert climbed the porch stairs and nearly ran into his Uncle John, who was backing out the door while balancing one end of the living room sofa.

"Watch out, son," he said.

Robert backed down the steps into the yard as he watched his uncle and father carefully maneuver the sofa onto the truck bed. He asked, "What's going on, Dad?"

The men leaned on the truck – both were perspiring heavily and out of breath. After what seemed like an eternity, his father wiped the sweat from his brow and said, "Son, how would you like to live in Buffalo?"

Robert froze. The urge to urinate vanished, along with all the sweet thoughts of summer, Plum Street and Colombia he had enjoyed up to a few moments before. He stared at his father and swallowed hard. "You…you…mean, we're moving?"

Cal Wexford glanced at his brother, then turned to Robert. "Well, son, you know that I've been working up there for the past five months, coming back here on the weekends to be with you kids and Mom. The car dealership was kind of giving me a tryout, and now they've offered me a full-time position as assistant office manager. It doesn't make sense to keep going back and forth now that I have the job for good. Mom and I've talked, and we think you kids will like it there. We'd like to move before school starts, you know."

Robert's jaw dropped and he felt overcome with panic. He glanced at his father, at his uncle, then suddenly felt the urge to vomit. Bolting past the two, he scurried up the stairs, tripped on the last step, and fell with a thud onto the porch. His father attempted to help him up, but Robert tore away from his grasp and ran inside the house.

That night, Robert refused to come out of his room. He ate nothing for dinner and later, he cried himself to sleep.

It took Robert several years before he pieced together the reasons for what happened that day. Eighteen months earlier, his father had lost his job as a bookkeeper at a local car dealership. Unable to find work and with a wife, three boys and a newborn girl to support, Cal traveled the 70 miles to Buffalo and applied at every dealership he could find. Several more months passed before he was offered a trial position as assistant office manager at a large downtown Chevrolet franchise. Cal rented a room and commuted to Colombia on weekends to be with his family.

The new opportunity restored the family's income stream but proved too little, too late for the bank that held the mortgage on their house. Cal and Anne Wexford had fallen behind on the payments and the bank took possession. Yes, they moved to Buffalo to be closer to Cal's work, but the reality was they had lost the house and were forced to relocate.

In spite of his parents' best efforts to paint the move in a positive light, Robert lapsed into a deep funk. His little brothers and the baby were too young to know any better, but he was all too aware of what he would leave behind. There would be no more games of tag, no more running into the kitchens of kindly old ladies asking for a drink of water or a cookie during play breaks, no more circuses starring all of his friends, no more fort-building on the hillside above the street.

But most importantly, he and his brothers would be leaving the only school they had known, St. Mary's. Founded in the 1940's as a mission school by Franciscan nuns from nearby St. Bonaventure University and housed in a converted garage on the outskirts of town, the institution provided first-rate education through third grade for local Catholic kids. Staffing it were two nuns, Seraphim and Francesca, who were biological sisters with thick Boston accents and no-nonsense attitudes. One taught kindergarten and the other first through third grades, positioning her desk in the doorway between classrooms. Younger kids learned more advanced concepts by osmosis, and the Wexford boys thrived in the atmosphere. But now they were leaving the comforts afforded by life in a small town for the big city.

The family's time in the Buffalo area was mercifully short. Cal found a rental in New Kensington, a blue-collar suburb north of the city. The house was nicer than the one in Colombia, but the neighborhood was rough-and-tumble. Robert was the runt of the block and ended up tagging along with older kids as they wandered the neighborhoods looking for pick-up games of tackle football. He learned quite a few new "words" in the process which he knew weren't allowed at home, and he was more than ready when his father sat him down a couple of months later to discuss the facts of life, having picked them up from his new acquaintances. The public school they attended was big and impersonal, a far cry from the cozy atmosphere of St. Mary's. Robert, David and Jimmy Wexford hated pretty much everything about New Kensington, and by Christmastime they were at the end of their rope.

Fortunately, that same month Cal was informed that the dealership had decided to expand to the Finger Lakes region about a hundred miles east of Buffalo, and he was offered the position of office manager for the new franchise. The Wexfords had been in New Kensington for all of four months but they would soon be on the move again, this time to the small lakeside city of Westport.

# CHAPTER

## 8

*The Present*

A few days had elapsed since returning from the Coeur d'Alene vacation, but Robert was still excited by the prospect of going back to Westport. Something tugged at him, a weird sense of calling or purpose that he'd never experienced.

"Maybe" was now in the rearview mirror, replaced by "when" and "how". Six weeks seemed to him about right for a time commitment. He also needed to figure out how to approach his physical therapy partners. He worked part-time and his schedule was tailored around the others' vacations, so some juggling would be needed if they gave their approval.

At dinner the following Friday, Robert announced his intentions to Ellen. He told her that he'd approach his group the following Monday at lunch and put in a request for a six-week sabbatical. He'd accumulated vacation time to cover part of the stretch, and he figured that the two recent associate hires would be able to take up any slack in his absence.

"Rob, don't you think you're taking a chance doing this?" Ellen asked. "Asking for this much time off when you're part-time to begin with isn't smart. It might prompt them to think about finding someone who's a little hungrier-looking to them than you. I mean, we're in decent shape financially, but you're not ready to retire yet."

"Look, they're my partners, I've worked with them for several years. They know me. It's not like I'm the new guy or girl asking for time off right out of the starting gate. I'll explain the situation; they'll know it's for a good cause. Elliott will understand." Elliott was the group's managing partner.

On Monday, Robert shifted around in his seat in the break room. He cast quick glances at the other partners as they ate their lunches and made small talk. Robert tried to gauge the mood before launching into his proposal. It seemed generally upbeat, so he decided it was time when a colleague asked what he and Ellen had done over the weekend.

"We didn't do much socially," he said. "But we did talk about a really important decision that I made last week up in Coeur d'Alene." The others looked up from their meals expectantly. He said, "Hey, I'm not retiring. Let's get that straight. But I might as well tell you. A difficult situation has come up back in New York State, where I'm from. My high school is in danger of closing, and they need four hundred grand to stay open. There's a fund drive…"

Elliott's booming baritone interrupted him. "Aw, $400,000 is chump change to you, Wexford. Write the check and be over it!"

The needling brought loud guffaws from those sitting at the table, and served to reduce the tension in the room. Robert's confidence was jump-started.

"Right. I actually sent them whatever I had in my wallet, and they thanked me for bailing them out," he said. "Seriously, I'm going to write them a check, but I see an opportunity to do something more as well. I'd like to ask the group for six weeks off to go back and help out with the fundraising or whatever else they want me to do. It's hard to explain, but a few things have happened recently that have kind of inspired me to do this. I know it's probably gonna be somewhat of an inconvenience to the rest of you, but I thought that the new staff were far enough along now to take up the slack in my absence. I'd be willing to cover for people if they want time off when I get back."

Elliott said, "Rob, there's a precedent for what you want to do." He pointed at another colleague. "Remember, he took that six-month sabbatical a few years ago when his father was on his deathbed in India. It was a bit of a strain on the group at the time, but we got through it. And as you say, our new people are coming along nicely and should be able to cover for you. These situations come up on occasion, and this one sounds more than reasonable to me. Of course, that's just my opinion. If anyone objects, speak up now."

The other partners agreed, and a couple of them commended Robert on his altruism. Robert felt himself puffing up a bit at the compliments.

Elliott said, "Rob, I have to ask you this. I'm not sure my wife would be thrilled if I up and left for six weeks."

Another colleague interrupted him and chuckled, "Ed, that's not what your wife told me." The retort evoked howls of laughter that brought the room down.

Robert smiled. "There *is* a bit of a disagreement about this with Ellen, but I'm...I'm working on her." He said it with more than a hint of embarrassment, knowing he stretched the truth.

# CHAPTER

## 9

"So," said Ellen. Her head was down as she pushed food around her plate that evening. "How did the meeting with your group go today, Rob?"

Robert pounced on the opportunity. "Pretty good, I'd say. I told them what had happened and what I wanted to do, and they pretty much gave me the green light. I've got six weeks, and I'll pay it back by working extra for anyone who needs it. And Elliott went to bat for me, too. I think that's what swayed everyone else."

"That's nice," she said as she stirred her food. "Do you think it was maybe too easy?"

Robert frowned. "What do you mean?" he asked.

"Maybe I'm a little paranoid, but you *are* a part-timer. And as I said before, maybe in their eyes you became a little bit more of a part-timer. There comes a point when people like that get kind of written off by their employers, you know."

"Come on, Ellen. I don't think that's the reason they were so willing."

"I'm not so sure," she said. "You still need to work. You aren't calling the shots anymore, like you did in Indianapolis. You work at their pleasure. I hope that they still value you the same as they did last week, before you asked them…"

His voice rose. "I'm as valuable to them now as I was a few days ago!" he said. "They know what I can do for them."

Ellen cleared her throat, which was usually her signal it was time to tap the brakes on a topic. She put down her fork. "I hope so. I'm just concerned about our finances. But I know you've already thought of that."

Robert assumed this meant that Ellen was in favor of his plan. He said, "I'll get on the phone with the travel agent in the morning and firm up a reservation. I can stay with Tilly for the first few days and then move into a hotel. I got a good long-term rate at the Hilton Garden down by the lake, and it's got a kitchenette so I can make most of my meals there. Believe me, I'm trying to do this in a fiscally responsible way."

Her green eyes flashed at him for a few seconds, and she then asked the question he knew would make him uncomfortable. "How much are you going to give them?"

He returned the stare for a few seconds. "I knew you'd ask. Obviously, that's a decision that you and I need to…"

"You know as well as I do that the final word on that comes from you." Her glare seemed to bore through him. "If I mention a number too low for you we'll have an argument. The number you have in mind is gonna be higher than the one I have, you know that. And what happens to all these donations if they don't reach their goal and they've spent a bunch of it on fundraising?"

"Tilly said they'd refund it on a pro rata basis. Do you think I'm that stupid that I wouldn't have asked that already? No one would shell out much of anything if they didn't have that assurance."

Ellen wiped her mouth with a napkin and tossed it on the table. "Tell me the truth. Who are you really doing this for, Rob? For them, for the school, for your hometown? Or for, you know, Rob Wexford? You *should* be doing it out of the goodness of your heart. And I know that you often have good intentions. But I hope you aren't thinking about going back there for a month and a half just so that your old friends will think you're such a great and generous guy. There's been a little of that from you in the past. I'm hoping you've grown out of that."

Initially feeling insulted, he then realized that his wife's remarks contained a kernel of truth. Yes, he'd had thoughts along those lines. But he so wanted this time to be different. "I think that what happened to

Alex and Alex were miracles, Ellen. And I believe that I found out about them the way I did for a reason. This *is* the reason. It's that simple."

Ellen smirked, gathered up her dinner items and rose from the table. On her way into the kitchen she asked, "How much of this is magnanimity, and how much is 'hooray for me'?"

He looked down at his half-eaten meal and slowly stirred it on his plate. "You want to know, Ellen? You really want to know? It's 80/20. And that's the truth."

"And which is the 80?"

CHAPTER

# 10

Robert gazed out the window of the plane as it took off from the Seattle airport. After a few minutes, the dreary low cloud cover of south Seattle gave way to bright clear skies and below, the rolling farmland of eastern Washington. He suddenly realized he was dead-tired, as the combination of a pre-dawn wakeup and several consecutive nights of fitful sleep hit him like a sledgehammer. He lapsed into a deep slumber interrupted only by the command to prepare for landing in Chicago.

Three hours later, after laying over in Chicago, he pulled his bags off the conveyor belt at Buffalo Niagara International and then walked to the rental car counter across the street. A few minutes after that, he was on the New York State Thruway headed in the direction of Westport.

As he passed some of the eastern suburbs of Buffalo, he was reminded of long-ago family trips to his uncle's house in nearby Alden for Thanksgiving, where he and his brothers would play football in the back yard waiting for the call to come inside and feast on turkey, mashed potatoes and gravy, dressing, pie and ice cream. After that, the men and boys would gather in the basement to watch the Buffalo Bills on television. How warm and wonderful those occasions were!

As he continued driving the pleasant thoughts of long ago were replaced by more sobering ones. Upstate New York was struggling economically and those struggles were apparent all around him, from the rusting cars passing by on the road to the ramshackle dwellings dotting the landscape. Decades of "tax and spend" policies had reduced the once thriving state to a shell of its former self. He pursed his lips at the thought.

An hour later, he passed the exit for Ganandoqua, the lakeside town twenty miles from Westport where his brother Jimmy and his family lived. Robert would be their dinner guest later in the trip, and he looked forward to catching up.

Half an hour later, he passed the sign that marked the city limits of Westport and proceeded to head down Commerce Street, the main drag. On the right stood St. Anthony's Church and its now-shuttered school, which had merged with Robert's grade school St. Anne's, on the south side of town. When Robert was growing up, this area around St. Anthony's was the Italian section of town. It still was for the most part, but the demographic was changing as a variety of other ethnic groups moved in. A couple of blocks later the neighborhood transitioned to downtown. On the right was a small grey building that once housed Vito's Bar, run by an eccentric but brilliant fellow full of stories and possessed of a memory so photographic he once greeted Robert, visiting the place for the first time in more than twenty years, by inquiring "Where the hell have you been?"

He noticed that the street had been widened since his last visit, with new sidewalks. Some of the downtown buildings had obviously been renovated. But Robert took note when he spied several familiar characters hanging out on the street corners, including Dickie, a cerebral palsy victim and downtown fixture still getting around on his specially-made oversized tricycle. His hair was now snow-white, but there was no doubt it was Dickie. The juxtaposition of new and old gave Robert cause to smile and shake his head.

He turned right and passed two red brick citadels – city hall and the post office. This route would take him to Tilly's and also give him a look at St. Anne's Church and its cross-street counterpart, Holy Angels Academy. He pulled up to the curb in front of the church.

The front entrance looked the same. Several brick pavers were missing from the sidewalk, and potholes dotted the side driveway, but the two signature pine trees were there, smaller than he remembered. They must have been replaced since his last visit years ago, he thought.

Shifting his gaze across the street, he was pleased to see the high school appeared to be in good condition. The stainless steel lettering above the front entrance still gleamed, the shrine of Mary that a classmate's father had constructed was intact near the front corner of the building and the trademark statue of an angel framed the side of the structure. The lawn was freshly cut, the landscaping immaculate.

*They may not have any money, but at least they're keeping the place up.*

He headed up the street, turned left, and spied Tilly's neat two-story, the second house on the right. Robert had called ahead from the car and he saw his friend sprawled in a rocking chair on the front porch, his feet perched on the railing.

Tilly stood as Robert got out of the car. "Hey."

"Hey."

This was the common salutation in Westport - nothing more, nothing less. The two men embraced and sat on the matching rocking chairs. Robert waited for the inevitable, and it arrived without delay.

"You wanna beer?" asked Tilly.

"I thought you'd never ask." They both laughed.

Tilly got up from the rocking chair and disappeared into the house. A minute later he emerged with four bottles of beer. "One for the road, one for the ditch," he said as he opened two of them.

"Thanks, Tilly. This'll go down in about three seconds. You get dehydrated on these long plane rides, you know."

"Welcome back, Rob. I can't tell you how much this means to me and to the school board. I've gotten some pretty nice feedback from people about what you're doing. You're making a big sacrifice."

Robert looked down. He was feeling his usual rush of self-congratulation but managed to suppress it. *This time it's going to be different,* he insisted to himself. "Yeah. Thanks, Tilly. It's a bigger sacrifice than you think. My wife is pissed about the whole thing. She doesn't think I've got my head screwed on. I told you what happened to inspire me to do this, but she's not feeling it. I kind of left Seattle on a down note, to be honest."

His friend frowned. "Really? I figured she'd be happy to have you out of the picture for a while."

Robert shook his head. "Funny you should say that. One of my work partners mentioned something along those lines when I asked for time off. Maybe you guys know more than I do about what's going on. Anyway, hopefully it's all temporary with Ellen." He was looking for a way to change the subject, and Tilly obliged him.

"Hell hath no fury like a woman scorned," his friend said, and he again rose from the rocking chair. "Hey, listen. Get your stuff inside and wash up. We're going to the Villa for dinner in 15 minutes. Gonna meet our buddy Herlihy."

Robert's face broke into a huge smile. The Villa was his favorite hometown Italian eatery. It was Saturday night and the place would be packed with locals. Plus, he looked forward to seeing his friend the old coach. He gulped the remainder of the first beer, balanced the other against his side and lugged the suitcases into the house. It was an unwritten Westport ordinance that one never left a beer unfinished, especially when you were the guest of a city councilman who wouldn't hesitate to make a citizen's arrest.

# CHAPTER

## 11

Robert watched out of the corner of his eye as Tilly struggled to pull the seat belt across his ample midsection while he simultaneously backed the car out the driveway. His new landlord had put on about 20 pounds since their last get-together a couple of years ago in South Bend. That, and a hairline in full retreat served to remind Robert that the years were piling up for both of them.

Robert's thoughts turned to his friend's many accomplishments. Tilly was a likable fellow who made friends easily and made sure he kept them. He didn't take winning his city council seat on the first try for granted. Instead, he worked hard to maintain his support and kept a finger on the pulse of his ward at all times. That was mostly a result of his trademark early evening walking rounds in the neighborhoods, taking advantage of a long-standing Westport after-dinner tradition whereby families would lounge on their front porches. Any concerns they had during these informal encounters were duly noted and followed up on by the councilman, either by solving the problem himself or by introducing the concern into the public record at the next council meeting.

As their vehicle made its way across town to the restaurant, Robert decided it was that particular attention to detail that he admired most in Tilly. They would need all of it and more in the weeks ahead, he mused.

He had another, more jarring realization. He'd been in town for hours but hadn't contacted Ellen to let her know he'd arrived in one piece. Robert pulled out his phone and started to text her before being interrupted by his companion.

"We'll have some company tonight, Rob. I mean, besides Dan Herlihy. Ron Alessia will join us - you know, the principal at Holy Angels. Also Father Donovan, the pastor at St. Anne's. Obviously both are on the school board. I thought it'd be helpful to get together with them tonight before the full board meeting on Tuesday.

"Sounds good," said Robert. "I've heard about both of them. And Donovan's brother, Jake, was in my class at Angels. I think he runs the funeral home over in Wellington now. Actually, the priest himself was in the class three years ahead of me, but I didn't know him then. Lowly freshman versus big-shot senior."

As the car approached the restaurant Robert gazed approvingly at the edifice. A converted residence, it still had the familiar blinking sign over the front door and the rear parking lot looked like it was already full. They found a spot for the car down the street, and a minute later Tilly swung the Villa side door open. No one ever used the front entrance. The irresistible aroma of Italian food complemented the kind of din that signaled an establishment flush with customers. Waves of hearty laughter punctuated the backdrop as working-class families enjoyed a night out on the town. Robert instinctively felt pangs of hunger, and he recalled Pavlov's Dog from science class, whose gastric juices were stimulated by the sensory perception that a meal was forthcoming.

Tilly mentioned to the hostess that his party had arrived. Their table would be ready in a few minutes, so they waded toward the bar to grab a beer. As they worked their way through the crowd several people called out greetings to the councilman.

Tilly chuckled when someone said, "I didn't think they let you out after dark!" Without hesitation, he followed that up with a few good-natured insults of his own.

Meanwhile Robert looked around the room straining to recognize a face, any face. All he got were quizzical looks from the patrons, the sort that hinted at vague familiarity falling short of outright recognition. Just as he was beginning to feel disheartened, he became aware of a firm hand grasping his shoulder. Turning, he met the smiling visage of a white-haired man with a Roman collar. Instinctively he said, "Father Donovan! Robert Wexford."

The priest shook Robert's hand with an iron grip. "You were in my brother Jake's class, weren't you? I spoke with him the other day and mentioned our dinner tonight. He said to tell you hello and to stay away from Tim O'Toole."

They both laughed heartily. Robert knew the priest grew up with O'Toole in the nearby village of Wellington. Tim O'Toole was a diehard "subway alumnus" of Notre Dame who now lived in Florida. He was another regular on the South Bend treks each fall.

"Trust me, Father. I try to stay as far away from that guy as I can. It's weird, but every time I spend a day or two with him, I wake up the next morning with a massive headache!"

This caused more laughter, because they knew the cause and effect in play; the cause usually related to John Barleycorn.

Robert said, "Father, is it true church doctrine holds that confession is in order every time one comes in contact with O'Toole?"

The priest was ready. "Not confession, my friend - excommunication! Anyway, my condolences on your relationship with the fellow."

Their name was then called over the loudspeaker, and the group made its way to the table. As they walked through the main dining room, more people called out to Tilly and Father Donovan. At one table, a man sharing a mildly ribald joke was elbowed by his wife as the priest neared. The priest had a look of feigned ignorance on his face. Tilly turned to Robert, smiled and winked.

A minute or two after taking their seats Dan Herlihy walked to the table, accompanied by another man Robert figured was Ron Alessia. After an exchange of greetings, the five of them took seats and Tilly ordered two bottles of Chianti, which was a sign the discussion would start in earnest.

"Robert, I understand that you took a few weeks off from your busy practice out there in Seattle to come and help us out," said Alessia. "No matter how this fund drive ends up, we all want to thank you for that great gesture."

"Thank you, sir," Robert said in as humble a tone as he could muster. *At least someone appreciates me being here.*

Alessia said, "Perhaps that'll serve as a jump-start for the fundraising, seeing how an alumnus is so concerned and committed that he would come across the country to assist. We need all the help we can get at this point. It's early May, we've got about seven weeks to go, and we're only at $70,000."

Robert's appetite suddenly vanished. He couldn't believe he'd neglected to ask Tilly how much had been raised so far. *How in hell are they going to come up with $330,000 in that amount of time?*

Robert looked down for a moment and then cleared his throat. "It sounds like we have our work cut out for us. I'm assuming that you've still gotta work through the rest of the major donors…"

Alessia cut him off. "We've already worked through the major donors, at least the local ones."

Robert shot a glance at Tilly, who stared into his almost-empty glass.

"You have to understand, this is Westport," said Alessia. "Maybe 50 years ago we had that kind of money here, at least in relative terms, but not anymore. We've tried to emphasize the promise we made, that all donations, less expenses, would be returned if the drive comes up short. But it hasn't had much effect. I think you're looking at a tapped-out community. And let me tell you, there's an undercurrent of opinion, and some are being very vocal about it, that maybe we should forget about the whole thing, capitulate, and let the school close."

Father Donovan leaned forward, by now cradling his second glass of wine. "Let me be clear what my position is and always has been. I have a fiduciary duty to the parish and to the diocese to tackle this problem in the most responsible way I can. Of course I want the school to stay open, all things being equal. No one values Catholic education more than I do. And more than anyone I've seen what that means to a community like Westport, how it's prepared citizens on both a moral and a civic basis. We've got seven of nine city council members including the mayor who are graduates of Holy Angels. Many in what's left of the business and industrial communities are graduates. But the counter argument is that a school one step away from closing, that's in long-term precarious financial condition, is going to sap the parish and the diocese. I don't want to sacrifice St. Anne's future for the sake of the school, and I hope everyone realizes that."

"We're with you, Father," said Tilly. "People may not have realized that early on, but I don't think that's a problem anymore. My opinion? The two board members who want us to give up and close the school now? They're the problem. We can't go out and ask anyone to help us if we can't even present a united front."

Robert looked at him in amazement. "You're telling me that the school *board* is divided on whether or not to even continue to *have* a fund drive? At this point?"

"Let's be fair," Tilly said. "The ones who want to close it are looking down the road, just like Father was saying. They don't want us to somehow squeak by on this drive, stay open for another year or two and then come back to the community with hat in hand for more. Their argument is that we need an endowment to ensure long-term stability. Nobody argues that. But the rest of us think that's a realistic possibility only if we stay open, if we prove our commitment. If we stay open, the thinking goes, we can go out and get a major donor, maybe someone like Dennis Richardson, to help us out with a really big gift."

"And manage that gift responsibly, not like we didn't do when the stock market tanked back in '08," added Herlihy.

Everyone nodded in agreement.

As their entrées were served, Robert's impulses got the better of him, again. "And I'd like to start things off by pledging $10,000 to the fund drive," he sputtered.

His dinner companions paused, some with forkfuls of pasta half in their mouths. All eyes were on the visitor.

"That's awesome, Rob!" said Tilly.

"Tremendous," said Herlihy.

Father Donovan stared at Robert in admiration. "You've already done enough just by offering to help out, and now you come up with this as well? God bless you, my friend!"

Robert beamed. *This is exactly what I'm looking for.* Recognition and adulation gave Robert a rush like nothing else. He was back on cloud nine but only momentarily. Like a Roman candle after reaching the apex of its course, he descended even more precipitously into an intense panic as he remembered he'd never discussed the specifics of a donation with Ellen.

His tablemates noticed the sudden change in their guest's demeanor. Tilly reached over and shook Robert. He asked, "Hey, you OK? Did you make a rounding error when you said ten grand?"

The table erupted in laughter, and the commotion snapped Robert out of his trance.

"Uh, oh. No, of course not. I'm good with ten grand. You've got it. Trust me. Hey, I'm not gonna run around and ask folks to help us out without doing something my — I mean, ourselves. You know, everything gets around in Westport, and if they don't see my — our names on the donation list, well, you know."

"Of course. Of course, Rob," said Alessia. "But you have to know that $10,000 is very generous of you and your wife and we appreciate the sacrifice, as I know all of the community will."

Robert looked down and struggled to cope with the conflicting forces tearing at him. After a moment, he lifted his head and was distracted by a vaguely familiar figure getting up from a table across the room. The attractive blonde was about his own age. She slung an expensive-looking purse over her shoulder and made her way to the exit accompanied by a man he didn't recognize. Robert turned to Tilly and asked, "Hey, who is that chick over there? She looks like someone I know, but I can't place her."

"Oh, that's Rhonda O'Rourke," said his friend. "She was in the class ahead of you at Angels. For a while, anyway."

Robert's eyes narrowed as he followed the progress of the couple. The Rhonda O'Rourke he knew from high school had darker hair and wore glasses, but there was no mistaking the facial features. He was impressed with the makeover. Her companion was handsome as well – tall with salt-and-pepper hair and a self-assured demeanor.

"That's right! I *knew* she looked familiar. I thought she was down south somewhere." Robert felt the alcohol kicking up his spirits. "I hope you don't mind, Father, but I remember my upperclasswoman looking quite different in high school. And the new version is a definite upgrade!"

The others immediately assented, including the priest, who smiled at Robert.

"Yeah, Rhonda moved back to Westport about ten years ago, Rob," said Alessia. "After Chemcor went under way back when, there was a lot of, shall we say, recrimination about what exactly happened. She felt it best to take a break and try her luck somewhere else for a while. So she moved down to Atlanta. Got into the real estate business down there and did very well. Moved back and got involved in the community – got on some committees, did good stuff, even ran for city council. Didn't win, but that's probably the result of the bad blood from the factory closing, you know. Anyway, she's built up this little conglomerate since coming back, owns a roofing company, insurance business, bought up a lot of downtown properties that she's trying to rehab. Done some good work all in all."

The conversation turned to the upcoming Holy Angels school board meeting. After a few minutes of discussion, the group exited the restaurant and walked to their cars. A soft early summer breeze whistled through the bud-laden branches of the elm trees that lined the street.

"Good to see you fellows tonight," said Father Donovan as he unlocked his car. "I expect all of you at Mass this weekend. Even you, Tilly."

The others laughed. Tilly was known for his erratic attendance on Sundays at St. Anne's. "I'll be there, Father. Don't worry," he said sheepishly.

The priest smiled as his got into his car and drove off, leaving Tilly and Robert alone.

"Tilly, remind me what happened with Rhonda O'Rourke again. I'm not recalling all of it."

His friend leaned against a tree and put his hands in his pockets. "Sure. Obviously you know Chemcor from growing up here. Big chemical plant down on the canal toward Wellington. Employed, oh, around 600 folks at one time, most of 'em from Westport. The O'Rourke family controlled it for many years."

"Sure, I remember," said Robert. "Who could forget the O'Rourkes? They were what passed for wealthy when we were growing up. I wasn't one of the cool kids in school but I did get invited a couple of times out to their house for parties. The big front yard, house had what seemed like millions of rooms..."

"Right," said Tilly. "We all hung out there at one time or another. The place was party central in grade and high school, for sure. Anyway, that plant was one of the mainstays of the local economy for decades. But about 30 years ago the wheels started falling off. Some of it wasn't the O'Rourke's fault – cheap foreign imports, too much regulation, labor costs going up. But maybe things weren't being managed very well either. And pretty much all the people who worked there had their retirements tied up in company stock."

Robert leaned against a tree and whistled. "Oh, man. One of the cardinal rules about investing your money. Don't put it all in one basket."

"Yup. When the company started losing accounts and the business was drying up, management told everyone things were OK and not to worry. And they kept telling them their best bet was to keep buying stock in the company. People should have paid more attention to what was really going on, but it's a small town and the plant was an institution around here, as I said. Nobody thought they'd go belly up. But they did. Without warning, the O'Rourkes declared bankruptcy and closed shop. Six hundred people were suddenly out on the street, with the company stock now worthless."

Robert shook his head slowly. "Yeah, and any chance for a decent retirement gone with it."

Tilly nodded. "Correct. So you could imagine what the atmosphere was like around here for the O'Rourkes. Rhonda was pretty much running the company at the time they declared bankruptcy, and she took the lion's share of the blame from the locals. She saw the light and figured it was time to get out and start a new life someplace else. And that's what she did."

"OK. So who is the guy she's with?" asked Robert.

"Some fella from Syracuse," said Tilly. "I think his name's Rick Vonderman or something like that, works for some kind of school outfit. They've been an item for a while."

Robert shrugged. "It's always something here in Westport, Tilly. Never a dull moment, I guess."

On the way home, Tilly suddenly slapped his hand on the steering wheel. "Hey, Rob – whaddaya say we have a brainstorm session tonight?"

"You mean to prep for the board meeting Tuesday?" asked Robert.

"Yeah. We've got a $330,000 hurdle in front of us. We gotta come up with a way to get over the top. Let's open a couple of pops when we get back and stay up until we come up with a plan."

Robert laughed. "Kind of like an all-nighter back in college. We didn't study for the test, so time to cram for it now."

By 4:30 am, the pair had exhausted the supply of cold beer in Tilly's refrigerator. Both snored loudly, the host on the sofa and the guest on the living room floor.

But they *had* indeed come up with a plan.

And they did show up for Mass a few hours later, although it wasn't a pretty sight.

# CHAPTER

## 12

Robert was grateful for Tilly's hospitality but had no intention of overstaying his welcome. He knew that Tilly's daughter still lived at home and commuted to college in Syracuse. She had been out of town visiting friends for the weekend, and Robert felt he needed to be out of the house. On Monday morning, he re-packed his belongings and left a note for Tilly that he'd return for a visit later in the day after moving to his new "home" for the next six weeks, the Hilton Garden Inn.

He had called for an early check-in, so after that he dropped off his belongings in the room and decided to shop for groceries. But he got no further than the parking lot. As he approached the car, his eyes caught sight of the familiar row of willow trees interposed between the lakeshore and the access road that also served as a walking path leading to the adjacent state park.

He stopped in his tracks after he realized that the parking lot stood on the very site where local youth congregated on weekend evenings long ago – a makeshift gravel lot known to every kid in Westport as Casey's. He had no idea why it was called that and very likely no one else did either. But it was everyone's meeting place on those hot, humid summer nights. Kids drove their parents' cars down here, parked and did what slightly errant small-town sons and daughters did at the time; drink and make out. There were dozens of neighborhood stores in Westport then. With as little as the blank ID card that came with a new wallet, enterprising teenagers could obtain refreshments from those stores like Country Club Malt Liquor. A Friday or Saturday night "special" consisted

47

of a few cans of "CC" topped off with a bag of potato chips or a couple of cheeseburgers from the nearest fast-food establishment. On special occasions, someone might show up with a keg of beer in a pickup truck and charge a dollar for all you could drink, thereby guaranteeing a *real* party would ensue.

As he reminisced about those impromptu lakeside parties, Robert realized something that only experience and adulthood could allow; the local gendarmes never arrested anyone at Casey's for what should have been obvious violations like underage drinking, open-container, or public intoxication. Now he knew why. The cops wanted all of the offenders in one place at one time! That way they could keep their eye on everyone, stepping in only when things got out of control. And a few fistfights here and there over a girlfriend or a school grudge didn't qualify as "out of control" to them. The police cruised through the lot in their squad cars a few times each night and intervened only if things *really* got out of hand.

And to be honest, they usually didn't. And to be honest, that was the way it was back then. Robert smiled at the thought of something along the lines of Casey's happening now. He laughed and muttered, "No way!"

He hopped into his rental and drove through the intersection across the busy highway separating the lakefront from the city. Robert turned left on Commerce Street, right on Oneida, and then headed up the hill toward the Methodist church topped with the iconic clock tower. After a few more turns, he was on Franklin, a half a block away from the house the Wexford family occupied for the bulk of Robert's time in Westport, a modest two-story clapboard set back from the street.

He pulled the car over and let the engine idle as he stared at his boyhood home. It was in much better condition now, probably the result of being owner-occupied. As renters, the Wexfords were at the mercy of the landlord, who wasn't much interested in maintenance. And at $125 a month, any requests for repairs were likely to be answered with a rent increase. It was difficult enough as it was to scrape money together to extend their stay another 30 days.

Robert looked carefully at the front porch. The steps were perfectly aligned and freshly painted, a far cry from the broken and unsafe condition they were in previously. Other memories came pouring forth as well – the dirt-floor musty basement, the chronically broken staircase banister, the stifling summer night heat in his tiny second-story bedroom. He glanced up along the side of the house at his old bedroom window. He was looking out that window one bone-chilling January night long ago when he heard a knock on the door.

"Son, it's your Dad. Can I come in?"

"Sure."

Cal Wexford sat on the bed next to Robert. "Son, I need to talk with you. You know I've been out of work since my heart attack last spring. Well, we've fallen behind on the bills and your mom and I can't seem to make ends meet. I hate to do this to you, but you know that money you've been saving for college?"

Robert felt his throat closing off. He had worked after-school jobs as a paperboy, grocery store clerk and printing company delivery boy in hopes of saving enough for at least one year of college. His grades were good enough to get into a decent private school and he figured if he got his foot in the door, he could apply for scholarships after that. His family was in no position to help out. He had put away $1200 in a savings account. He knew what was coming.

His father continued "That money can buy us time until I find work again. We're going to have to move out if I don't come up with back rent. I promise I'll pay it back to you."

Robert felt tears welling up but fought them off. "Sure, Dad." He walked over to his desk and pulled the passbook out of a drawer. "Here, take it."

He knew after his father closed the door that he'd never see the money again.

# # # # # #

Honk! He was jolted out of his musings by the blast of a car's horn behind him. He'd failed to pull completely off to the side and blocked the other vehicle's path. Robert waved apologetically to the not-so-understanding driver as he sped by and after making sure no one else was behind him, resumed his slow crawl down the street to the next intersection. Directly to his right was the old Westport High School, now empty and slated for demolition. Across the street from that stood his alma mater Holy Angels, and in the distance was St. Anne's Church.

But this particular intersection prompted even more memories for Robert. On the corner to his left was a dilapidated two-story structure. A small sign on the side of the building advertised it as a tattoo parlor. The familiar second-story overhang at the front was barely supported by two pillars covered with peeling paint and graffiti.

Robert inched the car forward, the front of the building now in full view. Back in the day, this was officially known as the Provenzano Grocery Store. To pretty much everyone in Westport, however, it was known as Eddie's.

# CHAPTER

## 13

Eddie Provenzano grew up like most Italian kids in the Butt End of Westport in the 1950s and '60s. He attended St. Anthony's Grade School and then Holy Angels, joined the military, came home and married his high school sweetheart. By the time he was 28, he and his wife were raising a special-needs son with twins on the way. His factory job wasn't going to be enough to support a growing family. And besides, he was bored with it.

In his youth, he'd worked at one of the many corner stores in Westport, the ubiquitous neighborhood groceries that dotted small-town landscapes prior to the advent of big-box retailers. Eddie had always harbored a dream of owning one of those places himself, but his dream had an added twist. He remembered the many high school classmates who ditched the neatly-packed lunches their mothers had prepared for them and instead headed downtown to eat at one of the soda shops and dairy bars.

He purchased a two-story building at the intersection adjacent to the two high schools with the intention of opening a store on the first level and using the second level as living quarters. Eddie had a hunch that a menu of pizza slices and homemade submarine sandwiches would satisfy the cravings of the hungry hordes pouring out of the two high schools up the street.

It was a genius move. The store was regularly mobbed with kids during the lunch hour and after school to boot. It quickly became the place where you had to be if you wanted to be "cool" – hanging out in front, wolfing down a sub or cold-square pizza slice, taking swigs from quart bottles of Orange Crush, joking and smoking. After school the kids reprised their lunch fare at Eddie's before heading home, then feigned illness or invented some excuse at the dinner table to explain away their curious lack of appetite. And the fact that the nutritional value of the "Eddie Diet" was, to put it kindly, substandard, was not a big concern at the time.

Eddie's was the place you met on weekend afternoons to plan the evening's activities. For those kids in the surrounding neighborhoods it served as sort of a community center, the place to go after school when homework was finished. Westport was home to dozens of large Catholic families at the time, some with as many as eight or ten children, often crammed into dwellings no more than 1500 square feet in size. Kids slept with three or four of their siblings in a single bed in an eight-by-ten foot room. So hanging out at Eddie's was *freedom*, and even more validating if your classmates spotted you with your hands in your pockets in front of the store while they were out for a spin in their parents' cars.

The crown prince of this little principality, of course, was Eddie Provenzano. From his throne on the stool behind the store counter, Eddie dispensed advice, settled disputes, offered counseling, and taught life lessons to his thousands of young charges, all the while overseeing the store operation. Eddie was a good 10 to 15 years older than most of his clientele yet he possessed an amazing ability to relate to them, becoming a de facto father to many. And he harbored no qualms about hiring them as employees, leaving the store in their care if he needed to run an errand downtown or tend to a family obligation. Counted among those he employed were the three Wexford brothers, who lived only a few houses away from the store. It was testimony to the respect the youth of Westport had for Eddie that none of them ever stole money or items during his entire time of operation.

And Eddie was keenly aware of the financial situations of many of the adult customers as well, with most of them living paycheck to paycheck. He kept a tab under the till, a small book where he recorded all credit transactions. At month's end those who could pay settled up with him, and those who couldn't were always given a reprieve, without interest being charged.

Robert chuckled as he sat in the idling vehicle and gazed at Eddie's old place. His thoughts turned to the many neighborhood characters who frequented it. Some of them lived across the street in a three-story, run-down apartment building known affectionately as The Palace. The structure was still there – definitely the worse for wear, he observed.

Robert's initial experience with The Palace was as a result of his very first job as a paperboy, in the eighth grade. He remembered forcing himself to breathe through his mouth as he made his way through its hallways delivering papers and collecting payment, in an attempt to avoid the overwhelming stench of urine and stale tobacco that pervaded the place.

One of the tenants was a fellow known as Sad Sack, so named for his permanent morose countenance. The Sack came in to the store every day after work, and his sole recurring purchase was two quarts of the local brew, Genesee Cream Ale. Big Lou was another tenant, a pleasant African-American giant of a man possessed of the deepest baritone voice ever heard in Westport. Lou would show up in soot-covered clothes after finishing work at the local foundry. And who could forget the immortal Mary Pontegrossi? She was morbidly obese with dirty, matted hair and barefoot. She'd appear at the store on her Jack Sprat-like husband's paydays sporting an ever-present cigarette hanging from the corner of her mouth. With a carbon-copy adolescent daughter in tow, she'd slap the paycheck down on the counter along with her purchases, usually consisting of a 12-pack of beer, bags of potato chips, and a couple of cartons of Winstons. Mary instructed Eddie or whoever was working to allow the child to take whatever she wanted from the candy rack. No one could ever recall the family purchasing any other items for sustenance.

Robert shook his head, still laughing, as he put the car in gear and drove slowly up the street as the old store receded from view in the mirror. The next four blocks on the left including side streets comprised his old paper route. This was the route that good friend John Patterson had bequeathed him after John got a higher-paying job washing dishes at the local country club.

Paper routes were good starter jobs for boys at the time but they were not without disadvantages. Negotiating the elements of harsh upstate New York winters on foot was one, and the income was wildly unpredictable to boot. As a paperboy you never knew how much you'd end up with on collection day, and if the total didn't meet the amount owed the newspaper the difference came out of your pocket.

And for Robert, there was the added problem of the rapport that the affable John had developed with his customers. Robert was a shy kid of few words, and he experienced more than his share of pangs of inadequacy as he struggled to match the standard of social interaction his predecessor had set. He recalled the lady in the dark green house who inquired when the Patterson boy was going to resume delivering her paper at every encounter with Robert for his entire two-year tenure.

When the car reached the next intersection, Robert glanced to the left at the houses that were on his route, then to the right. On the corner was the old Smoky Joe's store, now abandoned. Two houses down from that was a small brown two-story with a rocking chair on the porch. Robert swallowed hard as a feeling of unease welled up inside. Another memory from long ago came rushing back.

# CHAPTER

## 14

## *June 1965*

It was another steamy, sticky upstate summer afternoon in Westport. John Patterson was training his friend Robert Wexford to take over his paper route, and the pair had taken a break at the intersection of Franklin and Garden streets to buy sodas at Smoky Joe's store. The boys sat on the curb at the intersection, engaging in small talk and taking long slow swigs from their bottles.

Suddenly, they heard a commotion coming from behind them, followed by a loud *Bang!*

John jumped off the curb and pivoted toward the noise – it was coming from the brown two-story a couple of houses down the street behind the store. Two male voices were arguing, each directing streams of obscenities at the other in rapid fashion.

The front door of the house flew open. A grown man stumbled out, his arm in a vice grip around the neck of a boy who was about their own age. The man uttered another obscenity and slammed the boy's head against the porch pillar. The boy's head jerked backward from the impact and he fell in a heap onto the porch floor.

By this time the two observers had crept behind a small hedgerow on the side of the store to get a better view of what was happening. As they watched in horror the man picked the boy up, angled him sideways, and tossed him *off* the porch into the tiny front yard. The man muttered another unintelligible phrase, re-entered the house and slammed the screen door behind him. A woman's voice came from somewhere inside the house, followed by the thud of an inner door closing.

The victim of the assault slowly rose from the ground and pulled his T-shirt up to wipe the blood off his face. He had a mop of brown hair that fell like a curtain over his eyes. As he steadied himself, he brushed the hair to the side, revealing a sight that Robert would never forget – two small beady eyes flashed like those of a forest animal at night. The boy smiled weakly, in a sadistic kind of fashion, then slowly staggered down the street away from Robert and John. A strange laugh emanated from him as his figure receded from view. "Heh-heh-heh!"

The boys slowly straightened from their prolonged crouches and looked at each other. Robert felt a mixture of terror and amazement at the cold-blooded savagery he had witnessed. But John felt less so, as he had witnessed similar episodes previously.

"Who is that kid?" asked Robert.

John put his hand on Robert's arm and motioned for him to whisper.

"That's Danny Bouchette," he said in a low voice. They watched the victim stumble down the street. "There's only one thing to say about him – he's a badass! Stay as far away from that kid as you can. He'll corner you and pound the living crap out of you for absolutely no reason. I've seen him annihilate kids he doesn't even know, totally unprovoked, just for fun."

The boys walked back in front of the store, now out of sight of Bouchette, then headed down the street to finish delivering papers. Robert was still inquisitive. "Did that kid play junior football? I remember a kid named Danny on the Indians who was a good running back. He leveled one of the guys on our defense, knocked him out cold. All he had to do was run around him, but he purposely slowed and ran right over him. Scored the touchdown anyway."

John pulled a newspaper out of the bag, folded it effortlessly, and then threw it on the next porch. The paper slid magically to the front door, where it stopped. "My father wouldn't let me play junior football, but I have no doubt it was him. In Little League baseball, he was an All-Star, great power and speed. An all-around athlete, except with a bad attitude. He was always arguing with the coaches, disrespectful, breaking rules. Rules were for everyone else, not for Danny."

Robert fumbled with the newspaper that John handed him for the next house, still not adept at folding it correctly. "Can't imagine where he got the bad attitude." He laughed sarcastically. "Getting thrown off the porch every day at home will sometimes do that to ya!"

John smiled. "Absolutely. His parents moved here a few years ago from Canada – Quebec, I think. Lived over on a street next to the stadium. His folks disappeared and left Danny with his sister and her boyfriend - the guy you saw toss him off the porch. They're shacked up in that house. I think he's an alcoholic, 'cause he gets drunk and beats Danny up constantly. The cops have been up here a few times since they moved in."

John drew another paper out of the canvas bag, folded it expertly and tossed it on the next porch. Once more, the paper ended up directly under the front door. The two boys traded folding and throwing papers until they finished the route a few houses down from where Robert lived.

John grinned at his friend, and the dimple on his chin creased slightly in characteristic fashion. "Hey, Rob. Remember, Saturday is my last day. After collections, this route is yours. So, you think you're ready?"

Robert shrugged. He barely knew what he was doing. He wasn't totally sure which houses were on the route, half the time he folded the papers they unraveled when he threw them, and he had the distinct feeling that some of the customers weren't happy that an interloper was taking over for the popular incumbent. But he needed the job and the income that came with it. Times were close to desperate in the Wexford household and anything he could do to help out the family was a plus.

"I guess so," he said, aware that he was being less than forthright. "I appreciate you letting me take over. Gonna be hard to replace you, though. I hope the folks warm up to me at some point."

"Don't worry," said John in a reassuring voice. "You'll do real well. All of it'll click in pretty soon - you wait and see. Listen, I picked you because you're a good guy, polite, not a dummy." He paused and smiled.

"There's only one problem, though. I didn't want to tell you this until now, but you *do* realize that you live on the bottom part of the street, and I live on the top part of the street. That means that you'll be walking uphill every day with that heavy bag. I got to walk downhill!"

Robert was flustered. He was so naïve, the thought had never occurred to him. Even so, he feigned nonchalance and forced a smile. "Piece of cake, John. Piece of cake."

# C H A P T E R

## 15

*August 1965*

Two months later, toward the end of summer vacation, Robert was at the lakefront swimming with friends off the retaining wall near the state park. The sun neared the horizon, and he knew that meant it was time to cut the fun short and get back home to deliver papers.

He said goodbye to the other boys, walked across the highway into the downtown area, and turned left. One block later he turned right on Oneida headed toward the Methodist church with the clock tower. He had taken no more than 20 steps before he looked up and spied a couple rounding the corner at the top of the hill on his side of the street -a boy and girl about his age. As they drew closer, Robert's heart pounded. The boy's features were coming into view – shoulder-length brown hair, with beady eyes that glowered above a crooked smile.

Danny Bouchette!

Robert glanced at Bouchette's companion and recognized her as one of the hot girls his own age at Westport High. Gripped with panic, he stepped off the curb and crossed the street. When he reached the other side, he lowered his head as he walked up the hill, hoping against hope the bully would ignore him. Out of the corner of his eye he saw Bouchette mutter something to the girl, then step into the street toward *him*.

The coldest sweat of his life broke out on Robert Wexford's forehead, and his breath left him as well. For some reason, a momentary thought flashed into his head – something the Holy Angels school nurse had casually remarked during his freshman physical a week before.

*Five-foot four, 94 pounds.* He glanced down at his rail-thin, pre-pubescent frame, which served only as a sad reminder that he stood no chance against his taller and stronger antagonist. He closed his eyes in resignation as the executioner neared.

The girl called out. "Danny, come here!"

Bouchette turned around and slowly walked back to her, muttering as he did so.

Robert had slowed his pace considerably as the assailant drew near, but at the sound of her command, he looked up gingerly and caught sight of another figure approaching the couple from below, on their side of the street. It was a boy he didn't recognize, but he was about Robert's age. As the boy passed the couple in front of the theater, Bouchette reached out and grabbed him by the shoulder. Robert froze and looked on in horror as the bully slapped the boy a couple of times, then followed with a relentless series of body blows and head shots. The boy's pleas for mercy fell on deaf ears.

Robert stood, mouth agape, and felt an urge to go to the victim's aid. He hesitated for a split-second and then the nurse's fateful words came back to him. Filled with a mixture of shame tempered by the instinct of self-preservation, he resumed his walk up the hill. A few seconds later, he heard the familiar "Heh-heh-heh" coming from down the street.

As Robert reached the top of the hill he looked behind and saw the victim, writhing in pain on the sidewalk in front of the theater, blood covering his face. Bouchette and the girl headed in the opposite direction. The assassin had accomplished his dual objective of impressing his companion while satisfying his own twisted, sadistic impulse.

# # # # # # #

The idling vehicle was still parked in front of the long-abandoned store at the intersection. Inside, the grown man who still went by the name of Robert Wexford shifted uncomfortably in the driver's seat as he recalled the harrowing events from long ago – the initial encounter with

Bouchette behind the store and the vicious assault downtown in front of the theater. He was overcome with guilt as he thought of the poor boy lying in a heap on the theater sidewalk, bloody and semi-conscious. He'd turned his back on someone in need and run for cover, all to save his own skin.

*But he was also here to talk about it,* he thought.

*"Five-foot-four, 94 pounds."*

He took several deep breaths, gathered himself, and drove off.

# CHAPTER

## 16

As he had promised his friend, after grocery shopping and running a few other errands Robert headed back to Tilly's to hang out for the evening. Upon arrival, he found the front door ajar and walked in after a half-hearted knock. His former host was sprawled on the front room sofa and cradled a beer.

"You know you could've stayed here, Wexford," Tilly said lazily as he took a huge gulp.

"I know, Tilly," said Robert. "But I don't want to put you out for a month and a half, especially with your daughter coming and going. It's not right. Besides, if I stay that long, you might come to the same conclusion about me that Ellen…" He stopped in mid-sentence, shocked that he had uttered it. He didn't want his friend, who knew Ellen well and respected her, to be privy to any more of their marital difficulties than Robert had already divulged.

Tilly stared at him. "I'm sure you're joking, Rob. You guys have the perfect marriage."

Robert felt the air go out of his balloon but managed to recover. "Of course we do. I'm just putting myself down. It'd be detrimental to our friendship if you saw what I'm really like!" He laughed nervously, waiting for some signal from his friend that levity was in order.

"Don't worry," Tilly said. "I should have told Ellen what you were *really* like before you got married. It would have saved her a lot of grief! Now go in the kitchen and get two beers, please!"

Robert returned with the drinks and took a seat. The thought occurred to him that Tilly was lonely. Cancer had taken his wife ten years before, leaving a void that had never been filled. His response was to get involved in politics, initially as a campaign worker for others, then serving on city commissions and culminating in a successful initial run for city council. He was probably the most respected politician in Westport, even more so than the mayor. As a corollary, his insurance business was thriving. People trusted him.

Robert smiled slightly, grateful for the opportunity to work with his friend on the fund drive, knowing there was no other person in Westport who possessed his combination of inside knowledge and connection, confident that the fundraising plan they'd hatched two days before would succeed.

He slugged down the remainder of his beer and got up to leave. He had another thought before reaching for the door. "Hey, what say we grab something at Aunt Alice's tomorrow night before the school board meeting?"

Tilly nodded. "Sounds good. How about 6? Meeting's at school at 7:30. We can discuss strategy. We'll need to."

As Robert drove away, he suddenly realized that he had been in Westport for almost three days and had yet to speak to his wife. He pulled over and speed-dialed her number. After two rings, a familiar voice came on the line.

"Hi Rob." The voice was devoid of enthusiasm.

"Hi!" he said. "Thought you'd like to know what's going on here since I arrived."

"Sure," she said, without emotion.

"You don't sound real excited," he said.

"How would *you* sound if your wife just up and left you for some do-gooder mission a couple of thousand miles away?"

Robert felt the urge to respond in kind but resisted. Brushing off the comment, he gave his wife a detailed summary of what had happened since his arrival in Westport.

Ellen listened in silence until he finished. After an awkward few seconds, she said, "It sounds interesting – you've got a lot of work ahead of you. The kids say hi. You might want to call them at some point and fill them in, too."

"Oh, I will," he said. "Love you."

He waited for a response, but there was none. Instead, there was a dial tone.

"Crap! Dammit!" he shouted.

# CHAPTER

## 17

Robert surveyed the extra-large cheese and pepperoni pizza Tilly had ordered. It definitely had the look and smell of one of Aunt Alice's classics from the old days. Still housed in a small brick building almost directly across from St. Anthony's Church in the Butt End of Westport, Alice's had garnered a well-deserved reputation as perhaps the finest purveyor of pizza pies in central/western New York. The sagging ceiling tiles, stained from years of exposure to pizza vapors, and the adjacent creaky ceiling fans were unchanged since Robert's last visit years ago. Temperatures in the cramped space had to be north of 90 degrees as workers raced from kitchen to counter, brows glistening with sweat as they labored to keep up with in-house and to-go orders.

Tilly looked up after swallowing the first piece almost whole. "Now you know why I've got the gut," he said. "Hard to keep the weight off when you've got this kind of temptation a five-minute ride from your house. I come here every Tuesday."

"And head for the Villa every Saturday," Robert said. "If I moved back here, I'd weigh 300 pounds easy." He finished off his first slice and started to pull another one off, the thick rubbery white-cheese topping refusing to separate from the main body of the pie. "Tell me what's gonna happen tonight at the board meeting."

Tilly looked vacantly out the window for a few seconds before he answered. "OK. You've got nine board members, plus Ron Alessia, the principal, plus the diocesan representative. There's myself, Father Donovan and seven others. Of those seven, five are strongly in favor of keeping the school open, at least for the coming year, then trying to come up with a long-term solution after that. The other two want to let things go and close it now. Their position is as we had discussed– even if we come up with the money on the fund drive, it's going to be next to impossible given the economic situation around here to come up with a long-term solution. They say we'll be back before the community hat in hand by next summer."

He inhaled two more bites, washed them down with an enormous swig of Diet Coke and continued. "They have a point, but what the rest of us say is that's a defeatist attitude. OK, say we stay open this year and close next year. We've given this fall's senior class a chance to graduate from Holy Angels Academy. We think that's worth something. And you never know about a white knight coming in if we can stay open one more year."

Robert nodded.

"Now, on the other hand, those who want to fold this summer say we've lost enrollment, shed programs and activities, and it's time to face reality and forget about Catholic secondary education in a town this size."

Robert added glumly, "Kind of like Sisyphus rolling the rock up the hill."

His companion glanced at him and smiled. "Wexford, you sound like someone who…"

Robert cut him off before he could finish. "Catholic school, 1960s!"

Both of their faces lit up at the reference. They were proud of the education they had been so fortunate to receive in this small blue-collar city. Tilly took another swig of his drink and wiped his brow, which glistened with sweat. "Seriously, we need to deal with this rift on the board before we can proceed with any fundraising. We can't have some of us telling one story to potential donors and others saying the opposite. We've got to present a united front when we go out there."

Robert frowned, "I thought Father Donovan was giving mixed signals the other night at the Villa. What do you think?"

"You've got to look at it from his perspective," Tilly said. "Obviously as the pastor he wants to keep Angels open – he's a big proponent of Catholic education. But remember, the parish is on the hook for the building if the school closes. That's a huge financial albatross, what with maintenance, heating bills, and such. That's hanging over *his* head. And the market for a property disposition, if it needs to be sold, is fluid at best. If we keep it open for a couple more years, we may have trouble selling it then – again, depending on the economy and commercial real estate market. Who knows?"

Robert hadn't looked at it that way. "Who would buy it then? What would you use it for?"

Tilly shook his head. "I have no idea, Rob. It's a school, so maybe another education-related outfit would open there? But we don't know of any entity that would be interested at this point."

He glanced up at the clock on the wall. "Time to get out of here, pal. Time to go to battle! Tonight's the night we spring our plan on 'em!"

# CHAPTER

## 18

A few minutes later Tilly and Robert pulled into the school parking lot. Robert paused for a second before he climbed the front steps and looked up at the large, stainless steel lettering over the entrance - *Holy Angels Academy*. As the pair headed down the long, narrow first-floor corridor lined with student lockers, Robert was again reminiscing.

Tilly sensed it and slowed the pace in deference to his companion. They had a few "remember when's" as they passed old homerooms. The boardroom was actually a classroom at the far end of the first floor of the school. Halfway there, Robert stopped and told Tilly to continue without him.

On the left was his old freshman year homeroom. He pictured Sister Christine, no more than a couple of years removed from her profession of vows, at her desk patiently going over remedial Latin lessons with an after-school group. Ahead and on the right was the chaplain's office. Only two kinds of activities took place behind those doors. Either you were sitting around Father Hales' desk listening to one of his patented stories and laughing uncontrollably, or you were invited in for disciplinary purposes, in which case levity was conspicuously absent, and the priest's friendly voice morphed into something that sounded like a cross between a growl and a chain saw. All the more intimidating coming from someone who weighed north of 300 pounds and sported fists the size of grapefruits, which he didn't hesitate to wave ominously in the vicinity of the accused.

Robert's musings were interrupted by a rustling sound. He swung around to see an olive-skinned youth push a large trash receptacle toward him.

"Excuse me, sir. Could I get into that room behind you? I need to clean it up."

Robert was struck by how respectful the request was. "Sure, no problem," he said. It dawned on him that the boy might be a student. He had a thought. Up to now, he hadn't bothered talking to an actual *student* at his alma mater. This might be his chance. "Hey, son. Do you have a minute?"

"Yes, sir."

"Do you go here?"

"Yes, sir. I'm a junior."

"So, this is your after-school job?"

The boy seemed more than happy to converse. "Yes, it is. I clean up the homerooms in the evening. My family couldn't afford to send me here otherwise. It's not a bad job. I get to use the classrooms for studying after I get my work done. Too many distractions at home."

A faint smile of approval creased Robert's visage. He'd used empty classrooms for the same reason in college. He asked, "What's your name, son?"

"Francisco Suarez, sir."

"And what are your career plans, Francisco?"

"I want to become a dentist," he said. "I want to fix peoples' teeth so they can smile. I know too many people who can't smile because they're embarrassed. Some of them are in my family."

Robert was quickly impressed with the boy's sincerity and sense of purpose. "I'm not a dentist, but I'm in the health field. Physical therapy is my profession. It's been really good to me, and I love working with people who've been injured and are trying to recover. Very satisfying. And I know that dentistry would be similar in that respect. Good for you!"

Francisco broke out into a wide grin.

Robert said, "You know, I graduated from this place a long time ago. I'm back in town to help out with the fund drive. We'd all like to see kids like you continue to have a chance to get a great faith-based education that helps you get where you dream of going. I'm very impressed with your focus and determination." He fumbled in his pocket, pulled out a business card and handed it to the boy. "Here, this is my card. You or your parents can contact me any time if I can be of help."

Francisco accepted it and looked up at Robert with admiration. "This is wonderful! I'll show it to my mother and father tonight when I get home. Except I'll have to read it to my father in Spanish – he's only been here for a few months, and he can't read or speak English very well right now. But I'm working with him every day."

"Oh, so you've been here with your mother for a while?" asked Robert. "Your English is perfect, that's why I ask."

"Thank you. My mother and I have been here since I was 4. My father stayed behind in Mexico to take care of my grandmother. She had cancer. She died last summer, so after that my father came to be with us up here."

Robert frowned. "So sorry to hear that. At least now, you're all together again."

Francisco nodded. "Yes, he is very happy to be here. He got a job at the Villa washing dishes and keeping the bar stocked. When his English is good enough he wants to get a better job so he can make more money. Maybe I wouldn't have to help out so much by doing this."

Robert stared at the boy as the words came out. He thought of his own family situation while growing up in Westport; how he worked odd jobs to make ends meet at home, the grinding poverty that fueled his own desire to better himself. Francisco was *him!*

"Uh, are you OK, sir?"

"Oh, uh — of course," said Robert. "Just thinking of the old days right here at Angels! Let me tell you something. You keep on doing what you're doing and you will succeed in life, I promise you. Please tell your parents that they've done a great job raising you. You know, I'm going to go into that board meeting down there and tell them all about you right now!"

Francisco said, "Oh, that's OK. I think they all know me and my parents pretty well." He said this matter-of-factly.

Robert felt embarrassed. Again, he had allowed his self-absorption to get the upper hand. *Why did you think you were the only one on the planet who knows about this kid's situation?* He recovered somewhat. "Well, I'm sure glad to meet you, son. Remember, don't hesitate to contact me if you need advice." He shook the boy's hand and watched him resume pushing the receptacle down the corridor. It dawned on him that he was a good 15 minutes late for the board meeting.

# CHAPTER

## 19

As Robert approached the door to the makeshift boardroom his brow furrowed. He heard a number of people speaking at once; some in measured tones, others perilously close to shouting. It was obvious the board had a major disagreement on its hands, and given what Tilly had related to him that evening at Aunt Alice's, Robert was pretty sure it was about whether or not to proceed with the fund drive. He paused for a moment, took a deep breath and turned the door handle.

As it swung open, the chaotic din abruptly ceased; all eyes were on the stranger.

After a couple of awkward seconds, Ron Alessia broke the ice. "I'd like to introduce Mr. Robert Wexford to those of you who haven't met him yet," he said. "Rob is an Angels graduate who lives out in the Seattle area. He's taken a leave of absence from his job as a physical therapist to spend a few weeks here helping us out. He's got some interesting ideas about the fund drive – that is, if we decide to have one." As he said it he glared at a woman and man sitting together in the middle of the group.

A few of the board members made polite applause as Robert took a seat. Within a few seconds, however, the disagreement had resumed. The woman spoke first.

"We're going to spend money traveling around asking people for donations, right? And where is that money going to come from? It's going to come from funds we've already collected! That money is supposed to be used to keep the school open, not for travel!"

Tilly was ready. "Millie, the travel expenses are a necessary part of raising more money! I think everyone who's contributed realizes that you sometimes need to spend money to make it. "

The man sitting next to Millie said, "Well, that goes to my point, Tilly. Say we spend $10,000 or $20,000 trying to raise the additional money. But say we don't get to the $400,000 by July first. Now we're out that money, and we said we'd reimburse people if the drive failed. How are we going to come up with enough to repay them?" He slammed his fist on the arm of his chair.

Alessia said, "We've made it clear that we'd reimburse the money that's donated on a pro rata basis, which accounts for any expense incurred in fundraising. In addition, we have administrative funds that could help cover part of it if someone makes a stink."

The back and forth went on for 30 more minutes, and all the while, Robert sat silent, observing the participants carefully, sizing each of them up. Finally, during one especially tense exchange, he decided it was time to insert himself into the fray. He abruptly stood up and raised his hand.

"Obviously, there's a big difference of opinion here about whether or not to keep *my* school open."

Everyone sat in stunned silence at the remark. The visitor had managed to personalize the fund drive in a way that no one else had been able to do up until now. And the fact that their guest hailed from across the country made them all suddenly realize how wide the potential net was that Holy Angels *could* cast. Perhaps there were more people out there who cared enough, like this interloper apparently did, that they had overlooked.

Robert sensed it and stepped on the gas. "Hey, I walked through these doors tonight for the first time in many years. It was a very emotional moment for me. Lots of memories came back, the vast majority of them positive. I can guarantee you that there are hundreds more like me out there who feel the same way."

Millie's ally said, "OK, Mr. Wexford, I get that. I went here also, and I think I feel pretty much the same way as you about this place, although it's a little different because I live here in Westport and visit the school frequently. But where are all of these hundreds of alumni? Why aren't they breaking down the doors to help us now in our time of need? This place is broke. We've sent letters to the out-of-towners, but the response has been tepid to say the least."

Robert looked him in the eye. "You haven't asked them yet."

"But we *have* asked them."

"No, you haven't," said Robert. "You haven't *really* asked them yet. I looked you in the eye and said something to you. Do you think that would have had the same effect if I had written it to you in a letter? You – I mean *we* – need to go 'direct to consumer'. We need to sit down with them face-to-face."

Tilly nodded emphatically as his friend spilled the beans on one aspect of the plan they had hatched in the wee hours of Sunday.

Robert continued, confident that he now had the group's full attention. He moved out from behind his chair to the middle of the room. "I've been driving and walking around town the past couple of days. Yes, it's true that change is the only constant. But some things I'm seeing in Westport, I'm not liking. I drove past St. Anthony's last night with my windows down. Two kids were sitting on the church steps. One of them gave the other one the finger. And the other kid gave him a two-word, seven-letter salute. Right on the church steps! I ran into a cop downtown today. Crime is up, and he says respect for authority is down. Maybe it's a stretch, but do you think that shutting down a school that sends pretty much every graduate to college, that teaches respect for authority, the importance of charity and Christian values, is going to help fix that? By and large you don't see Holy Angels students or grads in the police reports. You've got seven of the nine city council members, including the mayor, who went here. Lawyers, doctors, teachers, the newspaper editor – they all went here. The fraternal organizations - look at them. Knights of Columbus, American Legion, the Rotary are all filled with graduates. Hey, I'm not knocking the public schools. But I *am* pointing out to you how valuable this institution has been to Westport. Step back and look at the big picture. We can't let this thing close!"

Robert exhaled and slowly made his way back to the seat. There was an uncomfortable silence in the room for perhaps five seconds, accompanied only by the buzz of the overhead fluorescent lights.

Father Donovan broke the ice. "Well put, Robert. Perhaps we needed an outsider to remind us how important the school is to this community, and has been for a long time. To say that we desperately need something like Holy Angels in today's social environment is an understatement." He paused for effect and then continued. "Everyone here knows I want Holy Angels to be viable. I speak for the other priests and for the parishes on that. My one concern is what I have already articulated to many of you– it's the parishes who will be left holding the bag if Holy Angels closes. Significant maintenance costs are associated with an empty building, especially in the winter with heating, pipes, etc. And if a sale of the property doesn't occur, there are demolition costs to deal with. So I have a sort of perverse interest in keeping the place open." He smiled as the words came out, but his statement provided some measure of much-needed comic relief.

Millie and her supporter had been engaged in a furious whispered discussion while all of this took place. A few seconds later she stood and spoke in a somewhat sheepish tone. "We've decided that, while we still have serious reservations about the whole thing, we think it best for the board to speak with one voice on the fund drive matter. We are willing to give our backing to it. We've got six weeks and $330,000 to go. Let's do it!" Prolonged applause followed as she took her seat. She smiled and stood again. "We'd like to qualify our approval. We back the fund drive as long as it's successful!"

Tilly knew this was the perfect opportunity to segue into an explanation of how the fund drive *could* succeed. It was time to take the wraps off the rest of the plan he and Robert had developed. He backed himself and his ample belly from the chair and rose to his feet, keeping his eyes fixed on his friend.

"Rob and I have had some discussions on how to get to our goal. Let me first say that it won't be easy, and it will entail some travel. But we think it's doable. We all know the local effort has stalled, probably in part because of our own difficulty in coming to a consensus, which is understandable. But now, thank God, we have that. What we've talked about is a two-pronged approach – local and out-of-town. Rob alluded to the out-of-town aspect. For the local part, we feel we need to do something different. And we think we have an idea that might work."

He circled the group, head down and hands clasped behind his back as he continued. "We need a catalyst for the local effort. That catalyst needs to be a community leader, someone who has local credibility, someone everyone in Westport respects. And we think we've identified that person. It's not a person who lives here. In fact he hasn't lived here for decades. If we can convince him to do what we envision I can almost guarantee it would raise a lot of money."

Without mentioning any names, he skipped to the second part of the plan. "Before I get to that, let me say that Robert and I think alumni and friends of the school who live in other parts of the country might have the deep pockets to help us make a dent in the rest of the capital requirement. Some live down South, some in the Midwest. Rob and I have volunteered to visit them for sit-downs, on our own dimes. We'll need to carefully plan for it, and that will take a week or two."

Millie smiled. "Well, I guess that addresses our concerns about travel. That's very generous of both of you. But I'm curious, as I'm certain the rest of us are. Who do you think this savior is who could rally the community?"

Tilly glanced at Robert and paused. "Eddie Provenzano."

As the words came out of his mouth, smiles and nods of approval appeared around the room. Someone said, "Absolutely brilliant!"

Tilly said, "He's living in Florida, hasn't been back here in years. But I guarantee if you went into any business, any bar, any restaurant, people know him. And if you ask what they think, everything they say will be positive."

Now it was Robert's turn. "I grew up down the street from his corner store. He was like a surrogate father to my brothers and I. All of us worked there growing up. Every kid in Westport knew him and respected him. If we can talk him into it, we'd like to host an appreciation dinner for him at the Little Italy Club. Invite all his friends, which means pretty much all of Westport. He'd be the guest of honor. Be upfront on the invitations that it's a fundraiser for the school, with a $300 donation pledge – half due at the banquet and half by July first. If we get 300 people to sign on, that's $90,000. And Eddie has way more than 300 friends!"

Tilly said, "We think that if a few of these out-of-towners come through, plus what we might make at the Eddie thing, we're looking at a large chunk of that $330,000. Maybe all of it."

A palpable air of excitement was in the room, one that had been depressingly absent from previous deliberations. The rancor of earlier in the evening dissipated, replaced by supercharged confidence. With a measure of reluctance, Ron Alessia motioned to adjourn the meeting at 10:30.

Several of the board members flirted with the speed limit on their way home and an extra measure of pep was present in their pedal feet. At last, things were maybe - just maybe - looking up for Holy Angels.

# CHAPTER

## 20

The board split into working groups in a final effort to raise any additional money they could from the local community prior to making an announcement about the testimonial dinner. Despite their best efforts, however, they were only able to come up with an additional $20,000.

Robert and Tilly finalized their plans for the out-of-town donor visits. And there wasn't much time to organize the Eddie event, either. Tilly made arrangements to reserve the Little Italy Club for Saturday, June 17th. Set smack in the middle of the Italian-American neighborhood of Westport, this city landmark hosted major talents such as Frank Sinatra and Nat Cole during Prohibition. Over the years, it had been transformed into a banquet facility and most of the wedding receptions and Westport civic events took place there. Tilly settled on standard Westport fare for the menu – ziti, chicken, sausage, meatballs, and salad. Given the importance the event held for the community he extracted a healthy discount from the proprietors, along with a promise to keep a lid on things until the school was assured of Eddie's participation.

That assurance would hopefully come next weekend when Tilly would fly to Florida to drop in on Eddie, using the phony excuse of catching up on old times while on a golf vacation. At the same time Robert would embark on his donor trip, starting in Florida, moving north to Atlanta, and ending in the Chicago area.

But before any of that happened, Robert needed to keep his dinner appointment with his brother Jimmy, in the nearby lakeside town of

Ganandoqua. Early the next Thursday evening, he pulled into the driveway of Jimmy and Nora Wexford's tract home in the picturesque community 20 miles from Westport. His brother had recently retired from
his job at Federal Express and was in the midst of starting a landscaping
business. Nora still worked as a manager at the local credit union. They
had two college-age children, and son James lived at home while attending the state university near Rochester.

James answered Robert's knock on the front door. His uncle gave a
stern look to the youth before breaking into a wide grin. "I was trying to
pull your chain, James! You know your uncle. Always expect the worst
when Uncle Rob shows up!"

Jimmy and Nora walked into the foyer. Robert looked at his brother
warily, then said, "I thought it was past your bedtime, Jimmy - almost
sundown now. Or is Nora letting you stay up because your brother is in
town?"

It was a typical opening line when two of the Wexford brothers met,
and Jimmy didn't miss a beat. "I'm surprised the nursing home out there
in Seattle let you leave town for such an extended period, Rob. Maybe
they're trying to tell you something."

A few more good-natured insults were exchanged before Nora ushered them into the dining room for the meal. It wasn't long before the
subject turned to Holy Angels and the fund drive. Jimmy grinned widely
when his brother told him about the plan to invite Eddie Provenzano.

"Great idea, Rob!" he said. "I can't think of anyone better." He
paused, then said, "And I'm sure it was all Tilly's doing."

Robert nonchalantly turned to James. "See how your father treats
me? It hasn't changed since the days down at Eddie's store. He gives me
no respect." He attempted his best Rodney Dangerfield-pulling-at-his-tie
routine as he spoke.

Jimmy said, "You know, most of us would have ended up with rap
sheets if it wasn't for Eddie. He was always there for advice and counsel."
Looking up, he said, "And all that Catholic education didn't hurt, either.
Speaking of which, we sure wish we could have sent the kids to Holy
Angels. But times are different now. Yeah, the commute would have

been tough and the kids would have had to separate from their friends here. But the major obstacle was cost."

Nora said, "The property taxes here are ridiculous because of all the flight of industry out of the state. The rest of us are left holding the bag, and it seems like every other person here works for the government in some capacity or other. So that's a lot of mouths for the tax dollars to feed. We couldn't afford the Angels tuition on top of that. And we know a lot of other people in the same boat – they'd love to send their kids to the parochial schools but can't afford it."

Jimmy frowned as he continued the discussion. "You know what happened to the tuition tax credit bill last year, don't you, Rob?"

Robert shook his head. "No, tell me about it. But something tells me I won't be surprised by what you're going to say."

His brother said, "Well, our governor, who himself was educated in Catholic schools, had a meeting with all the bishops and the cardinal last spring. He got up in front of them and promised that he'd get the bill through the legislature, that he had the votes this time. Then during the next few weeks, the teachers union got ahold of him and reminded him where his bread was buttered. The bill mysteriously died in committee. The bishops got back-stabbed. That's the only way to put it."

Robert shook his head emphatically. "Can't say I'm surprised."

# CHAPTER

## 21

After his flight from Rochester touched down, Tilly called Eddie Provenzano to inform him he was taking a break from his golf vacation to stop over for a visit. Tilly maneuvered the rental car onto the palm tree-lined street in an upper middle class section of Daytona Beach. He slowed to see house numbers and found the one he was looking for – a neat one-story with manicured yard and plantation shutters. One knock on the door was all it took for the host to answer.

"Tilly, how the hell are ya'?" asked Eddie. He ushered his guest through the house to a large screened-in lanai at the back. As soon as they were seated, a vivacious redhead appeared. She carried a tray with three ice-cold beers.

"Tilly, meet my wife, Marlene."

Tilly rose and shook her hand. It was instantly apparent to him she and Eddie were the perfect match. Eddie's first marriage to Rita had ended unceremoniously years before and many of his friends back home had hoped that the second time around would be a charm.

"It's so nice to meet you, Marlene," Tilly said. He smiled.

"And so nice to meet *you*," she said. "Eddie has talked about you and the others in Westport for so long. All good, of course."

Tilly glanced at his friend and decided to go "all Westport" at this point, "It *better* have been good, Marlene. We have ways of dealing with people."

Eddie laughed heartily.

After a few minutes of chatting about mutual acquaintances and back-home happenings, Tilly felt it was time to shed the pretense for his visit. "Eddie, old buddy. I'm not down here on a golf vacation. I came for a specific reason. I want to talk to you about something, something very important."

Eddie sat back in his lounge chair. His eyes narrowed, and his now-silver hair rustled in the soft late-afternoon breeze. He took another long swig of his Corona.

"OK, what's up?"

Tilly said, "You know about Holy Angels - about the possibility of it closing by July?"

Eddie nodded and said, "Tilly, I plan on donating."

"Eddie, that's not what we want from you. We want *you* instead."

Eddie frowned. "What?"

"Yes, we want you to come back and let us fête you at a testimonial dinner, a fund raiser for the school. It'll be a giant party in your honor, with the price of admission a $300 pledge to the fund drive, half due that night and half by July 1st. If enough people come, and we think they will 'cause it's you, we could raise around $90,000 from it. It's scheduled for June 17th, a Saturday night. All based on you sayin' yes."

Eddie fidgeted in his chair. "Am I going to ask them for money?"

"No. Like I said, all you have to do is show up, with your lovely bride of course. When they see Marlene they'll forget about you and throw money at her."

His hosts laughed as Tilly continued. "All you gotta do is get up there and tell people what the school means to you. We'll do the rest. Invitations will go out with pledge cards soon, so it'll all be taken care of by the time of the banquet. Whaddaya say, Ed?"

Eddie looked at his wife, then at Tilly. He ran his hands through his hair as he spoke. "You know I graduated from Angels. If it wasn't for that school, I'd have no education, and the store probably would have never made it. Probably half my business came from the high schools and probably 80 percent of my friends, too. Those were some of the best years of my life. It was like having 6000 children, except that when they were hungry they gave *me* money to eat! I felt a responsibility for you kids, though. But it was a pleasure, not a burden. Yes, I'll do it!"

An enormous grin broke out on Tilly's face. He couldn't resist one last bit of Westport humor, though. "Eddie, that's great! You know, I told you they'd show up to see you, but there's always the chance......."

# CHAPTER

## 22

At the same time Tilly and Eddie were meeting in Daytona, Robert's plane touched down in West Palm Beach. He had carefully constructed an appointment calendar over several days that would take him from West Palm to Sarasota, then to Atlanta and on to Chicago. He knew it was absolutely crucial to hit on every visit in order to make any significant dent in the drive's requirement.

He approached the task with the same attention to detail that had served him so well in his professional work. Each party had been contacted by phone well in advance, with Robert explaining up front what would be asked of them. None of the targets were unwilling to meet him face-to-face, which he felt was an encouraging sign.

And he had chosen West Palm as the first stop on the tour because he felt his chances of success were highest here. He'd start off with one of his best friends, Tim O'Toole.

It had been almost 40 years since Robert and Tim had met on the road between Wellington and Westport. A gold sedan had blown by Robert's ancient Volkswagen Beetle on a hot August afternoon and spewed gravel onto his windshield. Furious, he'd accelerated alongside the sedan and gesticulated angrily to the driver to pull over. Ready for a confrontation, Robert had emerged from his vehicle and noticed the Notre Dame sticker on the sedan's rear window. His animus morphed instantly to a desire to meet the stranger, whom he subsequently learned shared his interest in Irish football. O'Toole told him he had been a "subway alumnus" of the school since childhood and had already attended several home games. The pair struck a pact to meet up in South Bend that fall and a lifelong friendship ensued, with Robert, Tim, and others from Westport and Wellington getting together annually for a home game.

Tonight's rendezvous would take place at Tim's unofficial office – Mulligan's Irish Pub in downtown West Palm Beach. Robert looked forward to seeing his old friend and his wife, Kate, at what was rumored to be a gathering place for IRA fugitive types.

At seven o'clock on the dot Robert walked through the front door of the pub and immediately heard the familiar "Hey!" coming from his left. Tim and Kate sat at the bar, and each nursed a glass of Guinness. Next to each Guinness stood a frosted glass of Harp lager for their guest.

Timothy O'Toole grew up in the lower middle class section of Wellington, in one of several large Irish-American families in the village situated a few miles east of Westport. Most of those families sent their children to grade school at St. Mary's. Young Timothy and his friends proved to be all the schoolteachers could handle and it was rumored the nuns and priests threw their own personal kegger party on the occasion of the gang's eighth grade graduation, such was the degree of mischief that Tim and company had inflicted upon the place.

O'Toole married his high school sweetheart and took a job as an electrician in Westport. But over time his career aspirations changed, and the couple moved to Florida where he found a job at an electrical engineering firm. Long hours spent taking night classes gave him a working knowledge of the field, enough to land him a promotion to company salesman. A few years later Tim and one of the lead engineers struck out on their own. They designed airport lighting systems and the new startup became wildly successful. However, all that success hadn't gone to Tim's head. He was the same earthy fellow with the salty language and big heart that he was growing up, and he never forgot where he came from. Tim's persistence in the face of life's adversity was what Robert admired most about his friend.

Their initial 15 minutes of conversation were all about Notre Dame football – who would start at left defensive end, whether or not the five-star running back from New Jersey would sign a letter-of-intent, etc. Finally, during a lull Tim looked intently at Robert and pulled an envelope from his coat pocket. He pushed it on the bar toward his friend.

Kate smiled and said, "Well, open it!"

Tim said, "We don't want you wasting good drinking time asking questions. Go ahead, open it." He followed with his trademark quip, "La-da-vas, la-da-ving!" a cool-sounding phrase no one knew the actual meaning of.

Robert looked at them and slowly fingered the envelope. He broke the seal and pulled out a check. It was made out to "Holy Angels Development Fund" for $25,000. His eyes widened and then met Tim's. A little upstate humor was in order.

"Tim, is that all?"

O'Toole howled and toasted his wife and friend, taking an enormous swig from his glass. He placed the vessel firmly on the bar and nodded to Kate, who rose and disappeared around the corner. A few moments later she reappeared with two familiar figures in tow. On either side of her stood Annunzio Pasquale and Dieter Gearhardt. They were the next two people on Robert's appointment list -people he was scheduled to meet the following day in Sarasota. Both of them were close friends of O'Toole and Westport natives.

Robert was thunderstruck. "What the hell?" he asked. "What are you guys doing *here*?"

Annunzio removed the foot-long cigar from his mouth. "So, ya thought you were gonna see us tomorrow, huh?"

Gearhardt grinned widely and slapped Robert on the back.

Both of them took seats at the bar and ordered drinks from Allen, the reputed IRA fugitive who doubled as bartender. Gearhardt picked up where Pasquale left off. "Tim figured it was more efficient if we all showed up here tonight. This way the school can save on travel expenses. And besides, it 's a good excuse to hop on over to see everyone. Us Westport people need to catch up." He took two envelopes out of his back pocket and threw them down on the bar in front of Robert.

Annunzio grunted, "Those are for you, Rob."

Robert was in a state of disbelief. Here he was barely 10 hours into his trip and he was already making hay, with the prospect of more to come. He nervously fumbled with the envelopes. Each contained a check, each made out to the school development fund, each for $25,000. He lifted his head and let out a war whoop that startled everyone within hearing distance. He turned to the bartender.

"Allen! Another round for my Westport homies! Chop-chop!"

Later, with his friends several refreshments into the evening and deeply engaged in conversation, Robert leaned back on his barstool and surveyed the scene. Annunzio's perch groaned under the stress of his five-foot-seven, 300-plus pound frame, and the stool was in danger of collapse. His bald pate and aquiline nose bordered the huge cigar that dangled from the corner of his mouth. The other corner served as a funnel of sorts for the shots of ouzo he ordered nonstop from Allen. Here was a man from the Butt End of Westport who had dropped out of Holy Angels after his freshman year to join the local National Guard unit. He'd gone on to establish a successful local paving business before tiring of New York's high taxes and moving to Florida. There, he got into the construction business and installed sewer and water lines for housing developments. In the process he made a fortune. Rumors circulated about some of Annunzio's connections, and the fact that he was missing a little finger did nothing to dispel them. Still, he was another Westport guy who never forgot who his friends were, a fellow who could always be counted on for a loan or an employment opportunity.

Robert chuckled every time he recalled his favorite Annunzio Pasquale story. Annunzio was hosting a party on his yacht on the Florida Intracoastal Waterway. After a particularly long wait at one of the drawbridges, and after several pleas to lift the bridge went unanswered, Pasquale disappeared below and emerged a minute later brandishing a shotgun. A couple of blasts in the air from the gun were followed almost immediately by the familiar "tick-tick-tick" of the roadway elevating, as the attendant miraculously gained new insight.

Next, Robert's gaze turned to Dieter Gearhardt. Tall, with sandy-blond hair and typical Nordic features, he was reserved, polite, and the polar opposite of his buddy Pasquale. He had settled in Westport 40 years before and established a small business empire of car washes, storage facilities, rental properties and more recently, a winery that overlooked the lake. He and his wife had retired a few years ago and purchased a place in Sarasota, although they still maintained their lakefront home on the outskirts of Westport.

Robert knew that Dieter had no direct connection to Holy Angels and he wasn't even Catholic, which made his gift even more special. He couldn't help also feeling a little puffed-up about the early and substantial fundraising success he experienced so far. His ego reared its head once again as he envisioned a triumphal return to the next board meeting with more than the amount he was charged to raise. He found it difficult to dismiss the "white knight" fantasies that danced in his head, despite the recent resolutions he'd made to banish them.

After polishing off his fourth Harp, Robert stood and called for attention. "Listen up, you guys! Raise your hands if you're going to be there for the testimonial dinner for Eddie on the 17th!"

All hands went up.

"We've already talked about it," said Tim. He continued.

"You're probably wondering how the hell we all know about it so soon, aren't you, Wexford? You know word travels fast in Westport. And you know that half of Westport now lives in Florida, right? There's your answer. We're all staying at Dieter's place on the lake that weekend and renting a limo for the evening. We thought a pub crawl would be in order before the banquet. Just to get loosened up!"

Robert laughed. *Some things never change*, he thought.

# CHAPTER

## 23

Robert squinted and fumbled for the buzzing alarm clock in the dark hotel room. He was under the weather to say the least after the celebration at Mulligan's, and although he had the good sense to cancel his flight to Sarasota before passing out on the bed, he had completely forgotten to turn off the alarm. His head felt like it was going to explode, and waves of nausea gripped him.

He longed to lie in bed for a few hours to recuperate, but at some point he needed to rearrange the travel schedule, and he knew that would take up a considerable part of the day.

In the middle of contemplating it he shot upright in bed. "Gotta call Tilly! What about Eddie?" He grabbed the cellphone.

After two rings, Tilly answered. "Hey, Rob!"

Robert's voice croaked. "Hey, Tilly. Just checking in. How did it go with Eddie yesterday?"

The infirm tone of the question wasn't lost on Tilly, who had an inkling Robert was struggling. Tilly decided to take advantage of an opportunity to needle his partner. "Hey, you don't sound so hot. Either that means you had success yesterday and got hammered celebrating with the O'Tooles, or they shot you down and you tied one on because you felt sorry for yourself. Which one is it?"

Robert cleared his throat. "OK, OK. So I got rangooned, as Tim would say. That's gonna happen with that crew, be it good or bad - you know it. Tell me about your visit first, though."

"The eagle has landed, my friend. Eddie will do it – he's very excited. He says he's already working on his speech."

"Awesome," Robert said. "I have to tell you – we hit the quadrifecta! Not only did the O'Tooles come up with $25,000, I got a surprise sprung on me. The Sarasota boys showed up at Mulligan's and chipped in with the same amounts."

Tilly was ecstatic. "Holy crap! Listen, Wexford, if Eddie's dinner goes like we think it will and the rest of your trip comes anything close to last night, we'll have cracked this nut wide open! I'd say let's celebrate by having a drink over the phone, but I don't want to put you in the emergency room."

Robert smiled weakly. "I'm grinning, Tilly. That's all I can muster in my present state. Hurts too much to laugh."

# CHAPTER

## 24

Rick Vonderman pushed the hair out of his eyes and carefully tracked the nude outline of his girlfriend as she made her way out of the bedroom. He was too warm and comfortable beneath the tousled quilts to move. And besides, he and Rhonda had nothing of any importance scheduled for this lazy, late-spring Saturday anyway. He peered out the floor-to-ceiling window that faced the lake and caught the dim beginnings of the day's sunrise.

*What would possess her to get up this early?*

His curiosity was satisfied a few minutes later when Rhonda returned with steaming coffee cup in hand. She sat on the bedside with legs crossed and a towel over her ample breasts.

Rick jerked his head up and asked, "What the hell are you up so early for?"

She cradled her head in her hand. "You kept me up all night snoring. Probably all that wine we had to drink after dinner. You need to get in practice, darling. I'm a Westport girl, you know. We're good at holding our alcohol."

Rick dropped his head back on the pillow.

Rhonda laughed at him as she thought about the ingrained drinking culture of her hometown. *Then again, maybe that's the way it is in a lot of small towns. Then again, maybe that's the way it is in a lot of big towns, too.*

Vonderman glanced at his weekend roommate as she gingerly sipped her brew. "Hopefully in a year or two, I'll be here full-time and we can have a more normal life."

Rhonda looked blankly ahead as she faced the window. The light of dawn on the lake's eastern edge was increasing by the second. The long blond mane draped over her back tempted her lover. But she pretended to ignore his interest, took another sip of coffee and threw her head back.

Rick continued, "You said we'd be on our way to setting up shop here, but it hasn't happened. Holy Angels was supposed to be closed by now and it's still open. And now they've got this fund drive going. How much longer can we stand by before we need to make a move?"

Rhonda uncrossed her legs and stared him squarely in the eye. "Yes, I know. They surprised me by staying open this long. Who knows if they'll find enough money to stay open longer? We'll see. Even if they do, I've got something up my sleeve that may put a wrench in things."

"What could that be?" he said.

Rhonda smiled wryly. "You'll find out. Maybe we can talk about it tonight at the Villa over dinner. It'll make a good topic of conversation. Suffice it to say, if we're forced to do it and it works, there won't be any trail of evidence. It'll look like an act of God."

Vonderman laughed – the controlled variety, laced with a hint of bad intent. "Well, we've got to get the ball rolling somehow and soon. Time is wasting – it won't be long before the competition realizes what you and I already know. This place is a mother lode of opportunity for a vocational trade school. There's nothing like that within a 40-mile radius of here and there's hundreds of high school graduates in the area with no marketable skills. They get student loans, we get the money up front and we live happily ever after!"

O'Rourke grinned. "I know. We have to hope this fund drive flops. I hear they've got that puffed-head Wexford running around the country begging for money from alumni. He was always a nerd with an ego way too big for his britches. The school deserves to shut its doors. You know I have a score to settle with them."

Her companion nodded as his lips curled slowly into a cruel smile.

Rick and Rhonda preferred to eat their dinners at the Villa early, the better to avoid the customary Saturday night crush of patrons. At 5:30

that evening the couple strolled into the restaurant and took their usual spots at the far end of the bar. The wait staff made sure those seats were always available for them – O'Rourke was considered a Westport VIP, and she wasn't in the least bit shy about putting her surgically-enhanced features on display from her perch on the elevated bar stool, much to the male staff's delight.

After ordering drinks from the bartender, Rick turned to her and asked in a low voice, "Tell me about this contingency plan of yours."

She turned around and scanned the room to make sure no one was within earshot. As she did the kitchen door swung open and a short, dark-complected man with a tray of glasses appeared and headed their way. He smiled at the couple as he placed the tray on the floor and carefully stacked the glasses on the shelf beneath their seats.

Rick put his finger to his mouth, but she brushed him off. "It's OK. That's Manuel, the kitchen help. Speaks no English - trust me. You could say out loud right now that this guy stacking glasses is uglier than all get out, and he'd have no clue. I've tried to talk to him before and he understands nothing. They basically use sign language with him here. Just jumped the fence."

Somewhat reassured, Rick motioned for her to continue.

Rhonda took another sip of her Cabernet Franc. "You know I bought the roofing company a few years ago. You also know I own the insurance agency. It just so happens that I went through some of the old roofing records and it turns out the Holy Angels roof was put on by the previous owners of the business about 40 years ago. It's at the end of its useful life. I also came across a set of keys to the school building they had for the old project. Turns out the keys still work. I've checked the roof out a couple of times - obviously on the sly. It's a flat roof, the worst kind to have, and it's in bad shape. The capsheet, the covering over the plywood base, is wearing badly in several areas. It's about ready to separate in spots. All it would take is a few tugs and, voila, you've got huge holes. Loosen some of the plywood joints underneath, then wait for the June thunderstorms, which as you know can get pretty violent."

Vonderman listened intently but glanced nervously at the Mexican, who still arranged plates and glasses under the bar. To his relief the man still appeared oblivious to their conversation.

He looked puzzled. "OK, so there's water damage, but that's covered by insurance."

Rhonda smiled and waved her finger in the air. "Covered by insurance, you would think. But I told you that I own the insurance agency. And guess who dropped their flood insurance rider last year? Because they couldn't afford it anymore and had to cut corners?"

Vonderman flashed the same cruel smile and simultaneously shook his head.

Finished with his task, the Mexican got up and disappeared into the kitchen.

# CHAPTER

## 25

"Please return your seats and tray tables to the upright position as we begin our final descent into Atlanta."

Robert knew this second donor visit would be nowhere as straightforward as the first. He would need all of his not-so-considerable powers of persuasion to convince Fred VanHoose to participate in the Holy Angels fund drive. VanHoose was another member of the Wellington Mafia and a close friend of Tim O'Toole. Robert knew Fred's older brother from his time on the debate team at Angels, but he wasn't that familiar with Fred, who chose instead to stay in Wellington and attend the public high school rather than commute to Westport.

There were other mutual friends who grew up with Fred and who were still close to O'Toole. Chief among them were Mike France and John Cowan. Robert knew both and figured he could use these connections to carry conversation, at least for a while. But since Fred had no direct link to Holy Angels, it would take some convincing on Robert's part to coax him into helping out. He also knew Fred was perhaps his best shot for a really large donation.

Fred VanHoose was a math whiz in grade and high school and eventually obtained an accounting degree. He worked as a CPA for a Big Six firm in Tampa. One day he got a cold call from a couple that owned a small clothing store in town. They'd noticed some suspicious goings-on with their current accountant and needed a second opinion. Fred's investigation confirmed their suspicions and the couple rewarded him with their tax work. As the business grew and they opened additional outlets, they offered him the job of chief financial officer of the now-budding enterprise. He accepted and the rest is history. The small chain eventually morphed into Skirtz, the national women's clothing behemoth. VanHoose had cashed out and retired several years ago with a net worth in excess of nine figures.

Robert pulled up to the high-rise in the fashionable Buckhead area of Atlanta and parked the rental car. A few minutes later, he sat in the waiting room of Fred's charitable foundation on the 29th floor. Van-Hoose emerged from his office a minute later and extended his hand to the visitor as he grinned widely.

"Rob, how the hell are you? Is the headache gone yet? I heard you guys had a rough night at Mulligan's!" He blurted this out in front of the receptionist and another waiting couple.

Robert stammered and blushed, embarrassed. Obviously, O'Toole had called ahead. "Great to see you, Fred. Yeah, I'm recovered, but it was touch and go there for a while. Good thing I had a day to rest. You know the drill – you've been there many times with Hurricane Timmy!"

After being ushered into Fred's inner sanctum, Robert sat back in his chair and gazed out at the Atlanta skyline through the window framing his host. "Gee, Fred - nice setup. I should have gone into accounting."

Fred laughed. "Correction. You should have gone into accounting for Skirtz! I'd still be doing tax returns for little old widows if I hadn't taken that phone call. I lucked out."

"You're way too modest, my friend," said Robert. "Hey, look – let's get down to business here. You know why I came; we discussed generalities in our conversation last week. And obviously you've talked to Tim, so you know what happened the other night in West Palm. I could have flown up here under my own power after getting those three checks."

"Yeah, I know the whole story. Word travels fast in our little circle and I've been reading the Westport paper online, plus talking with old friends the past few weeks. You've got a deadline coming up and a tough nut to crack." He leaned back in his chair and stared at his Robert.

His guest saw the opening. "Well, what do you think? Have you made up your mind? Look, I know you didn't go to Angels but your brother did. Your family's Catholic. You went to St. Mary's grade school in Wellington. I'm thinking you value Catholic education."

Fred laughed. "Not when I was getting into trouble with Cowan, France, O'Toole and the boys in grade school! But I do now looking back. The structure and discipline were tremendous, and the quality of education was something you'd pay a private school thousands a year now to duplicate."

He paused and assumed a more serious expression. "I want you to tell me why I should donate, for this reason. Given all that has happened with their finances the past few years, how am I assured the money won't be pissed away again?"

Robert was ready for him. "Good question, and one that I myself asked out in Seattle a month or two ago. In fact, I threw the initial request for money into circular file pretty much for that same reason. But first let me tell you that anything you give will be refunded pro rata if the drive falls short. And second, I have an idea, one that the school board is also interested in pursuing. On a later stop, I plan to meet with a guy named John Casey in Chicago. He's a CPA like you - works for a consulting company there. I'm gonna try to persuade him to head up a financial review board for the school. It would serve as a checks-and balances mechanism for all future donations."

Fred nodded approvingly. "That's exactly what I was going to propose as a condition for my participation. So we're definitely on the same page."

Robert said, "Great to hear that. Beyond setting that up, we obviously need to dispense with stopgap efforts like this one and get an endowment going that'll serve as the school's financial underpinning for the future. That's the long-term goal but first we have to make sure we have a school to raise an endowment for. We're obviously in a bind. Can you help?"

Fred swiveled in his chair and looked out the window for a few moments. He pivoted abruptly and faced Robert. "I'm in. $50,000. Now get out of here and find the rest of it!" He smiled broadly. "Just kidding about getting out of here now. Let's go to lunch."

CHAPTER

# 26

Day 3 found Robert in Chicago. He had two stops in the Windy City. The first was with John Casey at his office on Michigan Avenue and the second was in the northern suburb of Evanston, where he would meet with Angels classmate Sue Piretti and her husband Sam, also a school alumnus.

At 12:30 sharp Robert sat with his mark in the boardroom of Casey's consulting company. John Casey was a Westport native who attended St. Anne's grade school and Holy Angels. Unlike Robert he had fulfilled his childhood dream of attending Notre Dame. He'd graduated with an accounting degree he later supplemented with an MBA from the University of Chicago. They had another connection as well, because their mothers had been long-term close friends.

After an exchange of pleasantries the two got down to business. "Rob, let me start off by saying that Sarah and I are happy to participate in the fund drive. We've talked it over. Holy Angels is very important to me. We believe in Catholic education – all three of our kids are in Catholic grade school here and we plan on sending them to St. Laurence for high school. So having said all that, how does $15,000 sound to you?"

Robert looked at him. Before he could issue the standard Westport salute, Casey had a retort, "Yeah, yeah, I know. Is that the best you can do? Don't even go there, Wexford. Get outta here."

Robert laughed. "You think you're getting off easy, my friend, but not so. Thank you for the generous donation. That's more than we expected and I know the school and the community are both very grateful. But I've got another request as well. How would you like to be the head of a financial oversight board for the school? It would address the concerns we've heard from people about how the school's spending its money. Apparently some are reluctant to give because of those concerns. I think you'd be as qualified as anyone to head that up."

"I was going to suggest that myself," Casey said. "I'd be happy to serve. I suppose I'd have to run it from here - maybe a trip or two a year to Westport, I would think. But it would be an excuse to get the kids and Sarah back there to see Mom, especially in the summer."

"We'd have no problem having those oversight meetings in the summer. And maybe during Christmas or Easter vacations," said Robert.

That evening, Robert sat down with the Pirettis for dinner at their favorite Evanston restaurant. Sam had started a successful computer software company 20 years prior. It was headquartered in Chicago. The couple hadn't been involved in supporting the school previously but it was apparent to Robert they were eager to start, especially when they heard about the possibility of the school closing. Robert brought them up to speed on what had been accomplished so far in Westport and on his current trip, and he let them in on the plans for the testimonial dinner for Eddie Provenzano. It seemed that was all they needed to hear, and at the end of the evening they had committed for $20,000.

Robert felt like pinching himself on the plane ride back to Rochester. This was too good to be true – in the past 72 hours he had garnered cash commitments from donors for $160,000. Throw in another $90,000 or so from the testimonial dinner and the local donations, which now approached $100,000, and they were within striking distance of their goal.

He gazed out the window and thought back to that first exchange at the board meeting with Millie and her friend. He and Tilly had been vindicated – where mass mailings had failed, face-to-face meetings had succeeded.

He recalled a story that his old Angels chaplain Father Hales had related about a man who fell away from the Church and was then approached by a friend about reconciling. The man accepted the invitation without hesitation. When the friend asked why he hadn't done so earlier, the man said, "Well, no one asked me."

He wasn't going to rub it in. But neither could Robert wait to walk into that next board meeting. *Hooray for me* never felt better.

# CHAPTER

## 27

A special Holy Angels board meeting was called for June 5th to finalize plans for the tribute dinner and to get a fundraising update. Robert had spent the past couple of days putting together a slide presentation summarizing what he and Tilly had accomplished on their recent travels. That afternoon Robert sat at his desk at the Hilton Garden and studied the slides he'd prepared for later that evening.

He reached for the last slice of day-old pizza in the box on the counter as he made his way through the slides, trying not to drop anything on his underwear. After he stuffed the piece into his mouth, he pushed the wire-rim glasses back on his nose and grinned. *This is going to be sweet*, he thought.

Until now Tilly and Robert had sensed that even though the board had seemed enthusiastic about their fundraising plan, an undercurrent of doubt still existed about its chances of success. Maybe it was learned behavior on their part, he thought, borne out of too many experiences where hopes had been raised, then ingloriously dashed.

But he meant to show them tonight that this time all of those misgivings were unwarranted. All it took was crafting a well-thought-out plan and executing it.

He got up from the computer, opened the drapes and looked out over the lake. *Yes – the native son triumphs, delivering the goods that will keep one of the pillars of the community from shutting its doors!*

# # #

Ron Alessia flipped the light switch back on. "Thanks, Rob. That was really good. Looks like we're on our way now."

Some of the others spoke likewise in appreciation of Robert's efforts. The mood in the makeshift boardroom was upbeat. Members even broached topics that had been considered off-limits, such as new faculty hires for the upcoming school year.

Unfortunately, not all was upbeat with Robert - he was crestfallen. Yes, the board had enjoyed his presentation. And yes, everyone appeared enthusiastic about the success of the fund drive. But in his mind the feedback was muted. He had worked so hard for so long to help save the school and *this* was the sum of their gratitude? He stared ahead while those around him busily engaged in conversation. *These people don't appreciate me.* He was fuming.

He'd come cross-country, foregoing almost two months of income from his job back in Seattle, leaving an unhappy spouse in his wake, spending a month of his time and effort in the community and flying around the entire eastern half of the country. And all he was receiving for the effort was a half-hearted "attaboy" from these ingrates?

*They don't appreciate me.* He repeated the phrase over and over under his breath for the rest of the evening.

# # # # # #

A few days later, Robert was running some errands downtown when he spied a familiar figure approaching. It was Rhonda O'Rourke. Robert felt an immediate sense of unease, and it was with some degree of hesitation that he extended a hand toward his former schoolmate as they slowed.

"Gosh, Rhonda – haven't talked to you in forever," Robert said.

"Uh, oh. Hello, Rob," she said weakly. Her hand returned a flaccid shake as she spoke. "I, uh, never got a chance to talk to you a few weeks ago at the Villa. I saw you at the table with all of the Angels bigwigs and didn't want to bother you."

Robert immediately knew this to be untrue but feigned ignorance. He also noticed that O'Rourke still had her childhood habit of speaking without establishing eye contact - something he detested.

Robert had gained experience dealing with people like Rhonda over the years. He decided to put it to use by setting his acquaintance on the defensive. "Hey, Rhonda. I should have come over to you first, because I did notice when you started to get up and leave. But I noticed you were busy with your friend. Who is the dashing stranger, anyway?"

Rhonda wasn't sure what to make of the comment – whether Robert was giving her companion a compliment or issuing a clever yet subtle putdown. "Well, yes. We've been dating for about a year now. Really nice guy from Syracuse."

Robert smiled, confident he had established the upper hand. "Really? How'd you two meet, by the way?"

The weak smile on O'Rourke's face evaporated. She was irritated at the line of questioning, coming from someone she barely knew now and hadn't spoken to in decades - someone she'd held in low regard from childhood to boot.

"Um, to be honest we sat next to each other at a real estate seminar."

Robert continued probing, enjoying his newfound advantage. "He's a realtor, eh?"

O'Rourke stiffened. "Well, not quite. He's vice-president of a firm that owns and runs occupational schools. It's headquartered in Syracuse."

Robert sensed his old schoolmate was desperate to switch gears, so he obliged. "I hope you're considering attending the tribute dinner for Eddie Provenzano next weekend. Sure would love to have one of Westport's VIP's there." He added jokingly, "Of course, all Holy Angels grads are required to come."

Rhonda's expression turned icy. "Come on, Rob. You know I didn't graduate from Angels. I moved over to Westport High my senior year. I hope you're kidding."

Robert froze, and his face instantly drained of color. He had totally forgotten Rhonda had transferred. She left mysteriously in the middle of her senior year to go to the public school. At the time rumors were she had committed some kind of serious transgression, but nothing was ever confirmed.

"I—I—I'm sorry, Rhonda," he said. "Yes, of course. My mistake."

She didn't hesitate to exploit the opening. "I hope things work out for you and the others on this fund drive. I'm sure you've done a good job – as good as you can do, considering what you're working with." She laughed spitefully. "Who knows, maybe you'll get the money. And maybe you won't!" Giving a tepid salute, she sauntered off.

Robert stood motionless for a few seconds, embarrassed that he had made such a gaffe and angry with himself for giving away the edge. He was stung by Rhonda's haughty putdown. But then the realization hit him that she had never really changed. She had put on a performance highlighting every personality defect that made Robert uncomfortable with her in grade and high school – the same pathologies that perhaps had contributed to her premature exit from Holy Angels.

"Why am I not surprised?" Robert muttered.

# CHAPTER

## 28

Monday before the testimonial dinner, Tilly scheduled a short meeting at the school with Father Donovan, Ron Alessia and Robert to go over final arrangements. The afternoon session would also give Robert a chance to observe the students during school hours, something he'd promised himself he'd do before his trip ended. The fund raising efforts had taken up much of his time, and as Friday marked the last day of classes it would be his only opportunity.

As he made his way down the narrow main hallway on the first floor the bell rang, and dozens of students poured out of the rooms on their way to the next class. This prompted Robert to lapse into another one of his dream states - imagining himself a student again, lugging impossible mountains of books between classes, laughing and joking with his friends, making fun of the teacher they had just finished with as well as the one they were about to confront.

He noticed the uniforms were strangely similar to the ones worn 40 years before – light-blue shirt and clip-on tie for the boys; blue plaid jumper and beige blouse for the girls. The flip hairstyles and horn-rimmed glasses were gone, but otherwise the students seemed the same. He winced when he realized how shy and withdrawn he was at their age, and how much it had held him back socially. He had worked diligently to overcome it, with some measure of success.

*Oh, man, how I wish I'd reached out more. Think of all the girls I could have...* That thought was quickly extinguished when he realized what he actually looked like 40 years ago – rail-thin, close-cropped hair, glasses.

He was a nerd, no question about it, a nerd with an outsized sense of self-worth to boot. *Oh, well.*

The bell rang again and those around him quickened their pace to get to their destinations. Conversations tamped down, as did his reminiscing. He regained his bearings and headed toward the principal's office for his appointment. On the way he passed a small office with its door partway open. He glanced inside and saw a rumpled, middle-aged man hunched over his desk as he scribbled on a notepad. Robert slowed as he hoped to recognize the face.

The man immediately looked up and squinted through thick glasses at the stranger in the doorway. He struggled to his feet and then almost fell over toward his left side before he grabbed the corner of the desk. Robert noticed his right eye was almost shut. "Excuse me, but aren't you Robert Wexford?"

"Yes, I am. And you are?"

"Salvatore DeDomenico. I was in the class behind you here."

Robert was shocked. He had known Sal vaguely in high school, but it was obvious something terrible had befallen him since. He gathered himself in an attempt to conceal his disbelief. "Sal, so glad to see you again. What are you doing here?"

As they shook hands DeDomenico again grasped the desktop to keep from falling over. He smiled. "Do you have a minute? Grab a chair and sit down."

Robert pulled a chair over and took a seat. "Sure! I've got a meeting in Ron's office in ten minutes to go over stuff for the dinner Saturday. But it's great to see you again, Sal."

His host leaned back in the swivel chair and laughed. "You ask what I'm doing. I work here part-time. My full-time job is with the county – director of social services. But my background is in psychology and counseling and that's what I do here at Angels. I'm here a couple of days a week dealing with teenage angst," he said as he laughed again. "Seriously, although it's a private school we do have some at-risk kids and they need help. Eventually I'd like to do this full-time, after I retire from the county."

Robert gazed at him in admiration. "I think that's wonderful. We need all the good people we can get here."

His host leaned over and looked intently at Robert. "I suppose you're wondering what's happened to me, the eye and the balance thing. Most people who haven't seen me in a while usually get around to asking."

Robert swallowed instinctively, and noticeably. "Gee, Sal. I, uh."

"No problem. I think you had gone off to college by then. It was my senior year."

# CHAPTER

## 29

*October 1970*

"Jeston is gonna like this one," mumbled Kevin Murphy to no one in particular as he finished typing in the Northside Stadium press box. He was putting the finishing touches on an article about the just-concluded Friday night football game between Holy Angels Academy and Wellington High School. Below him stadium lights illuminated the field, where volunteers were busily repairing the sod to make it playable for Saturday night's Westport High game. Remnants of the large crowd milled around, mostly family members or girlfriends who waited for players to emerge from locker rooms situated beneath the stands.

Holy Angels had prevailed in the hard-fought contest, which featured power running games on both sides, and a late field goal provided the margin of victory. More than a few bumps and bruises were inflicted - the kind of contest the old-timers in attendance had especially relished.

It was that essence of a "three yards and a cloud of dust" style of football that Murphy hoped to capture in writing as he proofread his story in the barren cinder-block structure perched atop the stands. He hoped that Ned Jeston, the sports editor of the *Westport Times*, would be pleased with it. Jeston had enough confidence in the boy that he'd assigned Murphy to cover any Holy Angels game that he himself was unable to attend. The Angels senior would drop his game summary off at Jeston's house later in the evening for editing, then count the hours until seeing his name on the byline in the next day's edition.

Kevin Murphy was a sports fanatic, and he was possessed of an uncanny ability to rattle off the most obscure statistic or factoid about any player in any sport, present or past. That gift combined with the education he had received in the local Catholic schools had been enough to gain the attention of people like Jeston. The boy's dream was to study journalism in college and eventually become a newspaper sports editor.

Sitting next to Murphy in the press box was his friend Salvatore DeDomenico, the official scorekeeper for all Holy Angels varsity sports. Kevin and Sal had many things in common – an encyclopedic knowledge of sports and significant physical limitations chief among them. Both boys were lacking in athleticism to say the least. Murphy disappeared from sight when he turned sideways and he wore thick horn-rimmed glasses. DeDomenico was short of stature and stocky, with a 100-yard dash time measured by sundial. And both were wildly uncoordinated. They had given up trying out for the various high school teams, each being without fail among the first cut. Fortunately they had discovered their calling in the press box.

A few minutes later the boys had gathered up their belongings and began the ritual post-game trek - initially to Jeston's house to drop off Kevin's article, then downtown to join their friends at the Mello-Cream soda shop.

They exited the stadium parking lot and walked down Oak Street in the direction of the editor's residence. It was a typical late-summer evening in Westport, with high humidity tempered by a lilting breeze that whistled through the hundred-year-old oaks lining each side of the street. The pair swatted at mosquitoes and flies that congregated under the streetlights as they made their way, laughing and joking, taking care not to trip over the uneven slabs of concrete that had been upended by tree roots growing beneath them.

This particular night was moonless and some of the streetlights were out, which made visibility less than optimal. The boys' feet made crunching sounds as they came down on the first dried leaves of autumn. Suddenly they became aware of additional crunching sounds - at first faint, then increasing in volume. Kevin looked around behind but saw nothing. They both slowed their pace but the other crunching sounds continued. Seconds later Sal made out three approaching figures, perhaps 50 yards ahead. At first walking, then jogging, the figures suddenly branched out – one to the left of them, one to the right, one staying on course directly toward the boys.

Kevin and Sal froze in their tracks, gripped with fear. The still-anonymous figures formed a half-circle, and then the middle figure emitted a sound that to this day still raises the hair on Salvatore DeDomenico's arms.

*"Heh-heh-heh!"*

As the figure to his right lunged toward him Kevin spun sideways. The perpetrator's hand grasped air. The maneuver gave him the split-second he needed to sprint down the street as fast and as far as he could, finally collapsing in the yard of a house several blocks away.

Sal wasn't so fortunate.

The three figures drew their half-circle tighter around him, and as they did he felt his heart in his throat. A cold sweat suddenly bathed his torso. The middle figure's visage came into view, just enough for the soon-to-be victim to make out two small, penetrating eyes that peered at him from behind a cut-out ski mask.

Seconds later a fist covered in brass knuckles shot out from the figure's left side. It crashed with brute force into the right side of Sal's face and temple, just outside the eye socket. He heard a crack as the force of metal on bone collapsed the eye socket inward.

Almost simultaneously the leftward figure slammed his brass-covered right fist into Sal's left ear. This blow was accompanied by a sickening thud.

The victim fell to the sidewalk, losing consciousness almost immediately. The three assailants hovered over their prey and after checking in all directions to make sure there were no witnesses, removed their masks. Two of them were identical with light complexions and short-cropped hair. The third - the one who struck the initial blow - sported shoulder-length brown hair. He let out a low guttural laugh and raised his hands in high-five fashion. The others obliged him, and then all three disappeared into the darkness.

It was almost 15 minutes before a remorseful Kevin Murphy, who had retraced his steps back to the scene of the crime, discovered his friend spread-eagled on the sidewalk. It was another 30 minutes before the ambulance arrived and rushed DeDomenico 50 miles to a Rochester hospital. An angiogram determined that he had suffered a subdural hematoma, or blood clot, around the brain, necessitating burr holes in the skull to relieve pressure. Two weeks later Sal emerged from his coma in the intensive care unit but it would be another four months before he returned to school.

The blood clot pressing on his brain was only part of the story, however. The initial blow to the right eye had also fractured the back of the socket through which the optic nerve passed, responsible for sight. The bony fragment had nearly severed the nerve, resulting in almost complete loss of vision in Sal's right eye. The second punch had fractured the bone of the inner part of his left ear in the area responsible for hearing and balance. The result was lifelong episodes of incapacitating vertigo and permanent hearing loss on that side. To top it all off there were additional fractures in his sinuses that left him with permanent nasal drip.

Neither Sal nor Kevin was ever able to identify the perpetrators with certainty, but they both had their suspicions, as did the Westport police. Danny Bouchette was the star running back on the Westport High football team, and he also had a well-deserved reputation around town as an incorrigible tough with previous run-ins with law enforcement. The Butler twins often accompanied Bouchette and the three of them had a history of street fighting in and around town. It wasn't unusual for those three and others to hop in cars and drive to nearby villages on the weekends looking to start a rumble.

All three were hauled in for questioning after the incident, but they denied involvement. With no witnesses and no evidence, charges were never brought.

CHAPTER

# 30

Robert listened intently as Sal related the terrible events of long ago. He thought of his own near-disastrous encounter with Bouchette in front of the theater as a freshman in high school, of how fortuitous it was he had escaped, and how the man now sitting in front of him had not.

He too had no doubt the attackers were Bouchette and the Butler brothers. At the time perhaps a handful of kids in Westport would have committed such an atrocity, and they were counted among them.

As Robert pondered this he noticed a tear running down Sal's cheek, and the weight of the entire situation hit him even harder. He also started to cry.

The two of them sat for a few moments, each quietly sobbing.

"I—I—I'm sorry, Sal," said Robert. "I am so sorry for this. It's the first I've heard of it. I haven't been back in town for any length of time since I left for college."

"Oh, that's OK," said Sal as he gathered himself. He reached for his handkerchief, moist and soiled from constant use, and dabbed it on his cheek. "No reason you should have known. It's not that big a deal to me anymore. Put it behind me, I guess. It's hard when I do have to re-tell it. Like when someone sees me and wonders why I look this way. Like now."

He finished wiping his face and continued. "The physical things, the physical things hold me back, but you have to keep going. Doing good things for others, that's what's therapy for me. The guy 2000 years ago showed us that. I try to take it from Him."

Unable to verbalize and overcome with emotion, Robert nodded. He paused and cleared his throat. "I saw Danny Bouchette beat the living crap out of a kid downtown when I was a freshman here. It was in front of the theater, to impress his girlfriend. It could have been me. I was across the street and he was coming for me, but the other kid got his attention for some reason. I know it was Bouchette in that group that beat you up. As for the other two, who else did anyone ever see hanging with Danny back then? It had to be the Butlers."

Sal said, "Oh, I know who they were. We all knew. But they were wearing masks. They said nothing before they hit me, so there was no voice to finger."

"Where are those bastards now?" asked Robert.

Sal smiled slightly as he said, "Mikey Butler was killed in a drag racing accident about ten years later. He was going about 110 mph out on County Road 6. His brother Stevie moved out west somewhere. I hear he's been in and out of prison. As for my friend Bouchette, last I heard he was down south. Guess what he does for a living?"

Robert shrugged.

"He's a boxing promoter."

At that, the two of them couldn't help but let out several much-needed chuckles.

Robert caught sight of the clock on the wall behind his host and realized he was ten minutes late for the meeting. He rose from the chair and extended his hand. "It's been wonderful seeing you again, Sal. You're an inspiration to me, as I'm sure you are to others. I only wish I had gotten to know you better in high school."

# CHAPTER

## 31

The door to Ron Alessia's office opened tentatively. Robert entered, apologized for his tardiness and took a seat.

Father Donovan turned and smiled. "Late for class again, eh, Wexford?"

Robert blushed. "Oh, yeah. I guess, Father. Actually, I ran into Sal DeDomenico before I got here. We were catching up."

Donovan's smile widened. "What a guy, huh?"

"You can say that again," said Robert. "I hadn't seen him since high school so obviously it took a while for him to explain things to me, if you know what I mean."

The priest nodded. "Yes, quite an amazing story and one that inspires me and all of us here in Westport. He's regarded as somewhat of a legend around here. Say, let's bring you up to speed on what's happening, Rob."

Alessia said, "We totaled up everything so far on the fund drive. As of yesterday we're at just under $280,000. That includes the $160,000 from your road trip and about $120,000 more from local donations."

Tilly said, "And I'm happy to announce that the dinner tomorrow night is sold out. In fact we've had requests for more tickets than we've printed. I just got off the phone with the people over at Little Italy and they can squeeze in around 30 more. So it'll be an overflow crowd – tables will be set up in the hallways to accommodate those folks. They won't be able to see anything from where they are but they'll hear what's going on in the banquet hall over the loudspeaker. I explained that, but they don't care. They want to be there to support the school and pay tribute to Eddie. Can you believe it?"

"It looks like we could clear about $100,000 tomorrow night, Rob," said Alessia. "You're a smart guy, you can do the math. We're very close to $400,000!"

Tilly leaned back in his chair and caught himself as he nearly tipped over. He folded two hands over his gut. "Looking good, my friends. Looking good. I think we've got pretty much everything covered. I'll pick up the Provenzanos at the airport in Rochester at 6 pm. I drop them off at Westport-On-The Lake where they'll spend the night, then pick them up again around 9 tomorrow morning. We take the grand tour around town and stop at places I know he'd want to see – the Butt End, his old barber shop, Aunt Alice's, etc. At 11, we give him a short tour of the school then head down the street to his old store. The newspaper and Channel 7 will be there for pictures and an interview. Then back to the hotel to freshen up, and we pick them up again at 6 and head for the banquet." He leaned over and picked up a brown paper bag from the floor. Out of it came a bottle of Chianti, a corkscrew, and four plastic cups.

Alessia rose and turned the lock on the door. It was time for a celebration.

# CHAPTER

## 32

Robert returned to his hotel room about an hour later. The wine had given him a much-needed emotional lift but now he started to come down again, and the funk that had enveloped him the past few days returned.

He flopped down on the bed and stared at the ceiling. *What the hell is the matter with me?*

By all rights he should be ecstatic. But here he was, near the end of a six-week pilgrimage to his hometown. He'd arrived to help his old school stay open. Now on the eve of the banquet, it looked as though that goal would be achieved. So he should be happy. Instead he felt an awful gnawing inside - an emptiness that was all the more overwhelming because he couldn't put his finger on why it was there in the first place.

He talked to himself in a low, measured voice. He often did this in times of trouble, acting as his own personal psychoanalyst.

*You started out behind the eight ball on this trip, Wexford. You and Ellen were on the outs before you even left Seattle and the way you left didn't help things either. Lots of loose ends and you never tied any of them up. No wonder you feel this way.*

*Yeah, but that's just the half of it. I'm pissed off at this place too. Here I am busting my ass for my hometown for a month and a half. Paying my own way here and on the road trip. Shelling out big money for the fund drive. And what do I have to show for it? A pat on the back is all. It's like they expected me to do it. What ingrates! How about a little love for the stranger who came from nowhere to help out?*

*Ellen's giving up on you, pal. In fact she may have already tossed in the towel. She has her own problems for sure. But yours are worse. You're a dead fish at home. There's nothing there and you can't fake it anymore.*

*This town isn't my town anymore. I hardly know anyone here. No one remembers me, I've got to introduce myself every time I meet someone, and they give me a blank stare when I talk about the old times.*

*Maybe it's your fault, Wexford. You didn't keep in touch, hardly ever came back to visit.*

*I feel like I'm in a play here and all the characters are interacting - except me. I wander around the stage and they go about their business like I'm not there.*

He punctuated the interlude by slamming his fist on the mattress and then jumped off the bed. He stared out the window at the lake and spied a small boat about half a mile off shore. A figure stood in the boat and cast a line into the water over and over. He sensed the scene was a metaphor for his current predicament.

The lake was Westport. Robert was the figure in the boat – surrounded by his hometown, but alone nonetheless - casting about, coming up empty again and again. He was so alone, so frustrated.

Then he inexplicably began to do something he hadn't done in a long time. It came out of the blue, without any premonition or premeditation.

He started to pray.

First the Our Father, then a Hail Mary, then nine more Hail Mary's, then the Glory Be - he had finished a decade of the rosary. Just as suddenly, he felt he had to stop. Rising and putting on a jacket, he walked down to the lobby and out the door with no clear idea what he was doing.

It was as if an invisible hand were pulling him.

To his right, across the parking lot, was the access road leading to the state park. Robert had often taken long walks on it during his stay at the hotel and he instinctively headed that way again. As he crossed the lot he craned his neck and peered out at the lake looking for the fishing boat he'd seen from the room. It was farther out now and moving south, probably headed back to its berth at some lakeside cottage.

A gentle breeze swept through the dozens of willow trees that lined the seawall between the road and the lake. Putting his head down, he walked briskly for a few minutes and then absent-mindedly looked up.

A woman approached from the opposite direction, coming out of the park. She was pretty, maybe 45 or so, with dark hair. They exchanged sterile greetings as they passed, then she abruptly stopped. "Excuse me, but aren't you Robert Wexford?" she asked.

"Yes, I am," he said. He didn't recognize her, but he was nonetheless pleased that *someone* out there knew who he was.

"You probably don't remember me. I'm Mary DeLuca. My brother Leo was in your class at Angels."

"Little Mary!" The words fell out of Robert's mouth before he could stop them. She was Little Mary to everyone back then because she *was* little, the kid sister of one of his high school friends. "Oh, I'm sorry, Mary. You understand, don't you? I haven't seen you since you were about eight years old."

She laughed, "Of course. You're not the first one to say that."

Relieved, he continued. "Well, not Little Mary anymore, but all grown up. Good to see you again. How's your brother doing?"

"Oh, he's very well. Has a good sales job down in Pennsylvania, married, two children. He doesn't get back here often, though."

Robert smiled and said, "You'll have to give me his address so I can hit him up for the fund drive. And how about you, Mary? What have you been doing since I last saw you?"

The smile on her face evaporated. She said nervously, "Oh, I moved to Florida in my 20s and settled there. Worked in the hotel industry for a while and moved back last year. I wanted my son to go to high school up here because – well, he had some trouble down there and I thought he could get a fresh start." Her voice trailed off.

After an awkward silence Robert broke the ice. "So you put him in Holy Angels, I assume?"

She smiled weakly. "That would have been my preference. But I couldn't afford it. He's over at Westport High."

Robert nodded. "I see. Where do you work?"

"Westport-On-The-Lake. I'm still in the hospitality business," she said. "My son is doing OK at the public school. But I still want to get him into Holy Angels if I can. He's a good athlete, leading rusher on the football team this past year. I talked to Dan Herlihy several times this spring. He said if the school is open next year there's a chance that Teddy could qualify for some scholarship money. Dan would love to have him at Angels. Obviously with the fund drive and all, everything is on hold right now."

Robert put his hand on her shoulder. "This is all sub rosa. But it looks like the fund drive is gonna reach its goal, and the school *will* be open in September. Your son must be a heck of a player for Dan to be that interested. He's a good friend of mine and a great coach."

"That's wonderful news," said Mary. Her face brightened. "I have to tell you, Teddy's had some discipline problems in the past, down in Florida and at Westport. I know mothers always say this but he really *is* a good boy at heart. He's had a hard life - grew up without a father, just me to keep him in line. I've done the best I could." She put her head down, and her eyes welled up with tears.

"I understand," said Robert. "We have a son also and it was difficult enough for him *with* a father around. A young man sometimes needs that hammer to drop once in a while, or at least the threat of one. Maybe Dan can get him into Angels over the summer and then things will turn around. You know, peer pressure is the most important factor at that age and peer pressure is positive at Angels."

As she wiped away the tears, Mary said, "It would be so great if that happened. And thanks for letting me in on the status of the fund drive. This will be terrific for Westport!"

The two parted, and Robert resumed walking toward the park. After a few more steps, he remembered the boat on the lake and turned to see if it was still in sight.

It wasn't, but as he stared out over the choppy waves, his thoughts turned to those fateful days a couple of months ago in Coeur d'Alene when he wadded up the letter from Holy Angels and tossed it away, the telephone calls hours apart from his friends about two people named

Alex, the conversation with the priest after Mass the next day about coincidences being occasions when God is telling us He's still around. His gaze suddenly froze, and his eyes widened.

*You idiot! That's why you're here in Westport. Not because you need someone to puff you up or tell you how great you are. It doesn't matter if you feel appreciated or not. You are not here to get something, you're here to give something. Give it and walk away. Your reward will come in time, in some other way, on another occasion.*

He instinctively repositioned his wire rims and as he was doing so, he recalled a passage from the New Testament. Something about doing good works in secret, with no acknowledgment, because the Father knows what everyone is doing at all times and will remember it.

He thought of all the times in his life he had done good works with the expectation of receiving positive feedback from others the only motivation for doing so. Then he thought of people like Sal DeDomenico, who had carried out countless acts of selflessness with no expectation of getting anything in return, all in spite of enduring horrible things earlier in his life. He'd just had an encounter with a single mother struggling to raise her son. Those were *real* troubles.

And he also realized how coincidence had affected *him* in his own life. He flashed back to his father walking out of the bedroom with his savings passbook, when it looked like there was no way he'd be able to further his education. In fact, a few months later Robert won a local scholarship competition that provided $1500 per year for all four of his years at Holy Cross. *Coincidence?*

A sense of profound regret enveloped him. He knew he'd promised to change at the start of this journey, and again at points during it, but he'd fallen into old habits in every instance. It was time to make amends. This was his epiphany.

A few minutes before, Robert Wexford left the hotel to take a walk. He returned from that walk a changed man - a different person, a better person, with no intention this time of going back.

# CHAPTER

## 33

Eddie Provenzano gazed out the window with nostalgia as the limousine wound its way through the streets of Westport's east side. This was home – the part of town that its overwhelmingly Italian population at one time referred to with not a hint of embarrassment as the Butt End. Although its demographics were now in flux it was evident from the well-kept homes and manicured lawns that community pride was still alive and well, an observation that gave Eddie much satisfaction. His children and grandchildren had long since moved to Florida to be nearer to him, and as a result it had been more than 20 years since he had been home. It was heartening after such a long absence to see the old neighborhood was doing well.

Even though the limo was still several blocks from the club both Eddie and Marlene noticed the streets were lined with parked cars. Eddie leaned back in the seat and stared at the ceiling as the magnitude of the occasion suddenly hit him. Alessia and Tilly had told him the day before that the event was oversubscribed, but Eddie couldn't recall any other Little Italy Club event where the side streets were as congested as this. When the car reached the entrance to the club parking lot a uniformed policeman stepped in its path and asked the driver for identification. Once he realized who the passengers were he stuck his head into the car and gave its occupants a thumbs-up.

"Eddie P! Good to see you, buddy! Remember me? Hasty Pudding from the store!"

Eddie gave him a fist bump and didn't miss a beat. "Hasty! Remember you? I've been trying to forget you and now you ruin it?"

The cop guffawed and waved them in.

The limo pulled up to the back entrance to the building and its doors swung open moments later. As Ron Alessia and the guests of honor emerged they heard the din of conversation and peals of laughter coming from inside, accompanied by the irresistible aroma of meatballs and sausage with an overlay of pasta gravy.

Ron turned to his company. "Are you ready?"

"I guess so," Eddie said. He glanced up at the sky and turned to his host. "Looks like one of our patented late June storms coming in." He pointed to a line of pitch-black clouds on the horizon.

Alessia nodded, "Good memory, Eddie. Yeah, it's supposed to hit later tonight - gonna be a big one, they say." A quizzical look came over his face. "Do you have your speech all set?"

Eddie looked bewildered. "What speech? You mean I have to give a speech? What is this?" He held up his arms and shrugged.

Alessia frowned. "You mean you don't have a speech prepared? Eddie, you've got 650 people in there who are expecting a speech! You cannot be serious that you don't have one."

Eddie gently put his hand on the principal's shoulder. He began in a measured tone, "Ron, I've never written a speech in my life and I ain't startin' now. But I've given thousands of 'em, mostly while I was sitting on my stool behind the counter at the store. My audience then was the same one I'm gonna speak to in that room tonight. I don't need no written notes." He pointed to his head. "And if I forget what I planned to say, I'll just make it up as I go along. No different than I've always done, see?"

Marlene burst out laughing and said, "Ron, don't worry. This is the way he does things. It always turns out well."

Alessia smiled wanly and gave his assent. Then he turned and knocked on the kitchen door four times.

A few seconds later, it swung open and a worker ushered them inside.

The plan was to sequester the guests of honor from the crowd until their introduction toward the end of dinner, so as to maximize suspense. At that point, the kitchen door to the banquet hall would open and Eddie and Marlene would make their grand entrance.

All of a sudden that same door flung open and Tilly lumbered through, decked out in a tuxedo and sporting a huge cigar hanging from the side of his mouth. He grinned widely as he caught sight of the Provenzanos. "Eddie P! Marlene!" he shouted.

After an obligatory bear hug and Italian greeting he removed the cigar and waved it in the air as he talked excitedly. "OK, listen to me! People are still milling around and getting gooned up. It's a real mob and are they excited! After dinner Frankie Pellitano will get up and go through all the introductions – priests, mayor, congressmen, board members, yada-yada. Then, he'll do his thing and work the crowd up before he introduces you two. At that moment we open the kitchen door, you guys stride up to the dais and take your seats. You're sitting in the center on this side of the podium, next to Father Donovan. And when you give your speech, Eddie, remember - plug the school!"

The blank stare reappeared on Eddie's visage. "What school?" he asked quizzically.

Tilly was ready. He slugged him gently on the shoulder as ashes simultaneously fell from the cigar onto Eddie's tux.

Eddie couldn't resist. "Hey, Tillie. Don't you know that smoking is bad for you? And I thought smoking wasn't allowed in here anyway."

"The fire chief is here," said Tilly. "There must be a hundred cigars goin' on in this place right now but somehow he hasn't seen any of 'em yet. Can't understand it. Come to think of it, he's got one too!"

Somehow, the ban on smoking had been conveniently lifted for the biggest event Westport had hosted in years.

Tilly did his best to wade through the wall-to-wall crowd ringing the huge circular bar in the front of the club. The bartenders worked furiously and tried in vain to keep up with the crush of orders from the wait staff mixed in with shouted pleas for more alcohol from those nearby. The air was thick with cigar smoke. Small groups of men emitted loud guffaws after the latest slightly off-color or politically incorrect joke was told, and women who took advantage of the occasion to dress to the nines were busily engaged in their own discussions.

Robert struggled to keep up with Tilly as they navigated the maze of humanity. His friend introduced people to him at such a dizzying pace he couldn't keep all the names straight. He had just finished talking to an old high school classmate he hadn't seen since graduation when Tilly tugged at his sleeve and pointed to the far corner of the barroom.

Robert elevated himself on his tiptoes, barely making out a large silver-haired gentleman holding court with a circle of about eight or ten others. The man was obviously relating a story, the listeners erupting repeatedly into loud laughter at various points in the telling. A few seconds later he turned halfway toward Robert and Tilly, revealing a Roman collar below ample jowls.

It was Father Hales.

Immediately Robert grabbed Tilly and the pair pushed their way through the crowd toward the rotund former Holy Angels chaplain and religion teacher. As they got closer the priest recognized them and smiled. Although deep into his story he paused for a moment to call out

to the pair. "Wexford!" he said, in keeping with his habit of using sur-
names with former students. "DeAngelo, couldn't you fetch me something better than this urchin?"

The group exploded in laughter again at this typical Father Hales
greeting, a mixture of gentle put-down and affection unique to the cleric.

Robert extended his hand. "Father, it's great to see you again," he
shouted over the din. "Are you still up in Rochester?"

"Yes I am," said the priest. "In residence, at St. Benedict's in Pitts-
ford. In residence means I just hang out." This prompted another round
of laughter from the group. He said, "Actually I'm still recovering from
my time with all of you delinquents at Holy Angels. I'm 30 years out
now and still not well."

Hales was a Holy Angels legend, a faculty member who spent a
good deal of his tenure driving around town in a station wagon on weekend evenings. He accosted groups of students he knew were up to no
constructive good and invited them inside for a spin, then kept them
occupied for hours with stories and bad jokes. Before they knew it they
were dropped off at their homes just before curfew. If they happened to
be inebriated, as was often the case, Hales drove around until they
sobered up, all the while dispensing subtle hints about the evils of drinking.

Robert smiled and continued. "You know, Father, you'd never get
away with doing that stuff now."

Hales nodded. "Oh, no question. I'd be strung up or at least
defrocked, given all that's happened. But you *do* have to admit that I kept
a lot of you out of trouble. Well, mostly out of trouble." Heads bobbed
furiously up and down.

The crowd around the priest gradually dissipated. But Robert
stayed, eager to discuss the strange happenings that prompted his trip
back to Westport. When the two were finally alone he related all that had
occurred, from Coeur d'Alene to the lakefront walk the day before. At
that point he found it difficult to continue as he described the events of
the day before, culminating in the personal tipping point he felt he had
experienced. His halting, quivering voice conveyed a clear message to the

priest that the entire experience of the past few weeks had left an indelible stamp on his former pupil.

Hales smiled knowingly. "That's not an unfamiliar story, Wexford - I've heard similar tales before. It amazes me that more of this doesn't make the news, at least for the inspirational aspect of it. But we live in a world filled with cynical nonbelievers who don't want to hear it. It runs counter to their narrative, which is that we're here alone, this reality is all there is, and we need to live for the moment. But I think the past two months happened to you for a reason. It wasn't coincidence."

*There was that word again.*

Robert flashed back to the words of Father Miles in Coeur d'Alene, but no sooner did he contemplate that than the priest standing in front of him interrupted.

"Wexford, I want to ask you something. You were kind of an arrogant little twit in high school. Some of your classmates took it for conceit. Have you ever grown out of that?"

Robert was shocked at the priest's bald assessment of him. His mouth dried up and he could feel the color leaving his face. "Well, Father. Um, thanks for the subtle criticism," he said with a bit of sarcasm. It took him a few seconds to recover, but he then felt a strange but powerful urge to unload some of the baggage he had accumulated in his life up to now.

"You know, Father, I think I *did* give off some of that vibe a little bit in high school. And unfortunately I don't think I've done a very good job of getting rid of it. But the fact of the matter is, maybe it was all a cover. I don't think I've ever had that great of an opinion of myself. I always felt like I was the underdog, the small kid, the poor kid, the one who wasn't good enough. Maybe I've been hiding all of it by acting another way. So, yeah, unfortunately for me, you're right."

Robert stared at his shoes and continued. "To be honest, I thought I was trying to use this past two months and everything that's transpired to rid myself of some habits that I've let go on for way too long. I keep saying that this time it's different but somehow I keep falling back into the same rut. Yesterday while I was walking on the lake path it finally, truly *did* feel different. I saw myself as equal to everyone around me - not below them, not above them. I'd never had that perspective before. Not sure why it took me so long but I'm eager to start over, to make up for the things I've done to others, especially my wife."

He stared into the priest's eyes. "It all changed for me yesterday on the lake path."

"You know, Wexford. What happened to you yesterday has all the hallmarks of a religious conversion." The priest smiled slightly.

Robert looked at him intently. "Seriously? Is that how it happens? I didn't really look at it that way."

Hales laughed. "Do you think St. Paul was thinking about becoming a Christian when he set out on the road to Damascus? A funny thing happened on the way to the persecution, my friend. Think about it."

Robert smiled. The old chaplain had nailed it - again.

After a few moments of awkward silence Robert remembered something else he wanted to bring up. "Father, I have a question for you. Maybe you don't know or don't want to say, but I've always been curious why Rhonda O'Rourke left Holy Angels in the middle of her senior year."

# # # # # # #

At that precise instant, a few miles away, Rhonda O'Rourke turned off her television. After the Weather Channel host disappeared from view she changed into a dark-colored outfit and donned a black knit ski hat. She picked up a backpack filled with tools, grabbed a portable light stand and plugged it into the garage outlet to make sure it was in working order, and loaded everything in the SUV.

As she maneuvered the vehicle down the winding driveway of the lakefront estate she craned her neck skyward. The weatherman had hit it on the number this time. Low-slung, pitch-black clouds pregnant with moisture were moving in from the west and the wind whipped ominously through the trees. She rolled down the window and took in a deep breath.

*The smell of rain - the first big June thunderstorm's arriving right on cue. Tonight's the night. What a crazy coincidence – unbelievably bad weather about to hit on the same day as the fundraiser. It serves them right, those bastards!*

She had called Rick a few minutes before to let him know it was time to implement the plan. Hopefully in a few hours she'd be back home monitoring the storm from the comfort of the sofa and savoring a victory glass of Cabernet Franc.

# # # # # # #

Father Hales' eyes widened at Robert's question. He paused and looked around, then spoke in a low voice. "If it wasn't for her last name Rhonda O'Rourke would have been expelled from Holy Angels long before senior year. From the moment she arrived she pulled stunts and acted like an absolute boor toward students and faculty alike. Her parents got her off scot-free every time, holding their status and money over our heads."

"OK, I get that," said Robert. "But what specifically happened to get her thrown out?"

The priest sighed. "Remember those slam books all of you passed around in eighth grade?" he asked.

Robert nodded affirmatively. "Oh, yeah. Boy, do I ever. Always worried what the other kids were going to say about me on my page."

The priest said, "She put one together on her own that was exclusively about one particular freshman girl. She invented all kinds of stuff about the poor kid making it look like it was something her classmates wrote. Then she put it in the girl's locker. When the girl read it she was devastated. She ended up having a nervous breakdown and eventually her parents moved from Westport so she could start over somewhere else. That was the final straw. We had a board meeting and it was unanimous – Rhonda had to go, money be damned. It was a shame in a way – I always thought she was extremely bright, perceptive with loads of potential. But she was permanently flawed by the circumstances of her upbringing, or lack thereof. I always knew where the first stop was on my Friday and Saturday night jaunts around town – the O'Rourke place. Because that's where all the kids were who were up to no good."

Robert said, "I ran into her downtown a few days ago. Made the mistake of thinking she graduated in the class ahead of me, and she let me know in no uncertain terms that she didn't. Obviously I haven't seen her here tonight, nor do I expect to."

Father Hales smiled. "I would have been shocked to see her too. I'm sure she holds a grudge against me. God bless her – I know she's done well financially since she came back from down south, but I don't know about what's going on between the ears. Like I said, it's a shame – someone who had all that going for her."

Someone's thick forearm cradled Robert's chin and slowly pulled his head backward. He spun around to find Dan Herlihy's bespectacled, crimson visage smiling at him. Robert greeted him with a symbolic punch to the gut, at the same time noting a man leaning on a cane standing behind the coach. It was Sal DeDomenico. Both intruders had obviously been fortified by their friend Jack Daniels and were in a mischievous mood to boot.

"Hey, Father. Look who we caught! He was in the girl's restroom looking under the stalls. Bringing him in here for some discipline!"

The chaplain was nonplussed. "That's the closest he'll come to getting any." The quip produced uncontrollable fits of laughter from all four of them.

Hales was pulled aside by another group of alumni, leaving Robert, Herlihy, and Tilly alone.

"What a great time to run into you guys," said Robert excitedly. "Yesterday afternoon I took a walk on the lakeside access road by the hotel. I ran into Mary DeLuca - hadn't seen her in forever. Dan, she said she's been in touch with you about her son. What do you think? Sounds like an interesting project."

The coach stirred his drink and adopted a serious air. "Listen. First of all, no one in this room is happier than me right now. We already had a hell of a team coming back next year, with four starting offensive linemen, depth and speed on defense, a pretty good quarterback coming up from jayvees. The only thing missing was a running back because we lost our top two to graduation. Now that we know the school will be open for business in September, we can go after this Teddy DeLuca as a transfer. There's scholarship money available and my friend the counselor here will go to work on the boy over the summer to try to get him to open up and heal. No question he's had some discipline problems but the Angels environment, along with Sal's guidance, will hopefully do the trick. Just talking football, the kid's a beast of a back – very physical, punishing style. He's compact but powerful, good speed, sheds blockers, and doesn't go down after initial contact. I love his style. But I also look forward to molding the kid into a responsible young adult."

Sal leaned on his cane. "Yeah, his style is to find someone to hit, even if there's no one around. Trouble is, up until now, he's used that style *off* the field as well as on it. That's what we need to fix, and we *will* fix it."

Herlihy drained his glass. "Yeah, his mom's a good woman. Had a rough time of it up to now, what with being a single mother trying to raise a kid with all of that anger and resentment spilling out. It'll be as good for her as it will for Teddy."

The trio raised their glasses in a toast and headed back to the bar.

# CHAPTER

## 35

The SUV pulled up to the service entrance at the rear of Holy Angels Academy. Rhonda flipped the ignition off, unloaded the backpack and light stand, then parked the truck a block away so it wouldn't draw the attention of anyone who might drive around the building while she was on her mission. Returning to the entrance on foot, she fished out the keys she'd stumbled on while cleaning out a desk at the roofing company months before, and gained entry. The stairwell to the roof was located behind the stage at the far end of the school gymnasium. She flipped on the flashlight as she made her way through the building to the gym.

No sooner had she turned the deadbolt on the rooftop door at the top of the stairs than it flung open, propelled by the strong gusting wind serving as harbinger of the monster storm predicted for the next 24 hours. She secured the door and unloaded the contents of the backpack. Anticipating the strong winds, she had brought along weights to fix the legs of the light stand, which itself would be necessary to locate the weakened areas in the capsheet cover of the roof once it turned completely dark.

O'Rourke had made three prior surreptitious trips up here and had also staged a complete dry run two weeks before, simulating every move she would make tonight. The preparation had her confident she was as ready as could be for the task at hand. On the dry run, she had marked with chalk the four locations where she needed to work, choosing low-lying spots where the 40-year-old capsheet was paper-thin. She'd already poked small pilot holes in the covering to locate seams in the underlying plywood sections. Those were the seams she needed to loosen and lift to allow the storm to do its job.

Three of the spots were in the middle of the roof and the fourth was adjacent to the low wall ringing the roof's perimeter. She would begin her task in the middle areas.

# # #

The familiar sound of the Little Italy Club dinner bell echoed through the hall at precisely 7 pm – the signal for the attendees to make their way to the tables. Robert was supposed to sit with Tilly and a group of his city council friends and their spouses at Table 10 near the dais. As he neared the table he saw three couples and an attractive-looking auburn-haired woman with her back to him. He made his way around to the far side and introduced himself but got no further than the first "How do you do?" before he was interrupted.

"Aren't you going to sit with me, Rob?"

The voice came from the opposite side of the table, so he glanced in that direction.

*Ellen!*

Robert's eyes widened, his jaw dropped and his mouth was agape. Then a voice boomed out behind him and a large hand grasping a very-used cigar fell on his shoulder: Tilly.

"Thought I'd set you up for the evening, Wexford."

Robert gave his friend a momentary squeeze and ran around the table. In order, he flashed his wife a huge grin, gave her a warm embrace and planted a wet, sloppy, embarrassing kiss on her lips.

The men at the table averted their eyes, the women looked on with glowing approval.

Ellen turned from the spectators as tears streamed down her face. "Oh, Rob. I'm so happy to see you again. I've missed you so much."

A happy yet quizzical look appeared on his face. "You - you have?" he asked.

"Yes. I can't explain now, but since you've been gone I've thought a lot about us. I've neglected you for a long time. I thought I had a fatally flawed husband, but now I realize I have a great husband with a few flaws. There's a big difference. It got to the point where I only wanted to see the bad. No more."

Robert held her by the shoulders, still in shock. "Wow. Wow! If it means anything, *I've* had a lot of time here to think about things. Ellen, I want to start over too. I'll fix the flaws, I promise. Weird things have happened, ever since the weekend in Coeur d'Alene and now here. I can fill you in later. But from now on I only want to give to you. I don't want anything in return. I've finally figured it out. I'm serious."

After embracing a bit longer the couple took their seats. Robert was still mystified by the logistics of his wife's appearance. "How did you get here? When?" he asked.

"Tilly did everything," she said. "He called me a couple of weeks ago and invited me to the banquet. I didn't say yes right away but that's when I started thinking seriously about things. He said he could tell that I was needed here. Anyway he picked me up at the airport this morning. I stayed outside in his car until the dinner bell rang, for it to be a surprise." She stared at Tilly and smiled. "You know, he'd make a great marriage counselor."

# CHAPTER

# 36

The Provenzanos were getting antsy. They had run out of people to talk to among the kitchen help and both of them felt like chickens in a coop. Eddie paced up and down the aisles as he waited for the signal to enter the banquet hall. He heard the muffled voice of Frankie Pellitano regaling the audience with stale Italian and Irish jokes from his well-worn repertoire. Eddie knew all of them by heart because they were the same jokes that had been floating around Westport for decades. Nevertheless something about Frankie's delivery still elicited the desired response from whatever crowd he attempted to humor. Tonight was no different, as guffaws and howls of laughter followed the punchlines that everyone knew were coming.

Eventually Frankie's voice assumed a more serious tone as he started introducing the VIPs in attendance - local and state politicians, congressmen and women, business leaders and clergy.

When he'd finished reeling off the names of the Holy Angels board of directors Eddie knew it was almost time. Pellitano paused for a good 30 seconds before launching into his patented introduction style, which started with his voice in a low growl. First came a synopsis of Eddie's life story – the humble beginnings on the east side of town, his first job as a grocery clerk, his dream of opening his own place, ending with an emotional description of Eddie's contribution to the welfare of the community during his time at the store. With each sentence Frankie dialed the decibel meter up a little more, until his voice finally reached a crescendo. The kitchen doors swung open and Eddie and Marlene strode through.

"Ladies and gentlemen, I give you the one, the only, Eddie Provenzano and his beautiful wife Marlene!" Everyone in the house stood and gave the guests of honor a prolonged ovation as they took their seats on the dais. With an overhang of blue cigar smoke and catcalls raining down from all corners, the atmosphere more resembled that of a prizefight that had concluded with a knockout.

Seconds later a worker emerged from the kitchen. He carried a tray covered with items everyone instantly recognized. Peals of laughter accompanied its presentation to the guests of honor – a foot-long cappacola submarine sandwich, a large section of cold-square pizza, a chunk of moldy cheese and a two-liter bottle of Orange Crush - the lunch menu for high school students at Eddie's store.

Eddie grabbed the sub and soda. He held them high in the air as the crowd clapped rhythmically in approval. He then yanked the microphone from its anchor on the podium and made his way to the front of the stage. He was emotional, as were many in the audience. After he wiped away the tears, he launched into his off-the-cuff speech.

"Thank you, thank you so much for all of this, from Marlene and me. First, I wanna thank the people who brought me here tonight– the great Tilly DeAngelo, the board of directors of Holy Angels and everyone involved in the fundraiser and at the school. What a great cause and what a privilege it is to be involved in it this way!"

"I'm very aware that folks paid a good penny to be here tonight. You should all be proud of supportin' the school, an institution that has been an anchor of our community for a hundred years. Ya' never throw away the anchors!" This drew another prolonged standing ovation.

He looked in the direction of Father Donovan and smiled. "Maybe I'm speakin' out of turn here, Father, but they tell me that if everyone who showed tonight pays up, this fund drive is over the top!" A third standing ovation ensued.

Eddie was really feeling it now. "You all can do the math. We'll see at least a hundred grand come outta tonight. That's a lot of money. Hell, that's almost as much as the unpaid balance on the tab that I had at the store!"

The crowd roared and many patrons had looks of resignation on their faces as they realized Eddie was probably referring to them specifically. "I'd like to personally thank every one of you for coming out tonight. I could say Joe this or Mary that, but we all know that's not the way we do it in Westport."

He looked out over the audience and put his hand up to his ear as he shouted, "*And how do we do it in Westport?*"

As if on cue, everyone knew the answer, and they shouted it back to him in unison. "*Nicknames!*"

Eddie nodded in approval and pulled a crumpled sheet of paper from his tuxedo pocket. Unfolding it, he growled into the microphone, "OK, when I call your name I want you to stand. Spouses too. When I finish with this list I'm comin' around to pick off anyone that I forgot or left out. When that's done I promise you there won't be many of you left seated!"

He started with the group most familiar to him – the neighborhood kids who called Eddie's store their second home. "*Creature! Fonzie! Sabe! Wally! LeeRoy! Hambone! Crazy Eights! Chizzer! Mucus!*"

Next were those who frequented the store with regularity but didn't live in direct proximity. "*Liver! Butts! Butthead! Asshead*!" A few of these drew pained expressions from the priests in attendance. *Amos! Wire!*"

Each name elicited the same response– a mixture of catcalls, good-natured ribbing, and occasional applause. And there was no lack of familiarity with any of them. In fact some in the crowd asked their friends for the person's *actual* name. In Westport there were those with nicknames, and then there were the outsiders.

Eddie proceeded to tick off the rest of the names on his list. "*Stump. Zo. Gus. Rocky. Wheezer. Fifi. FooFoo. Cork. Stavros. Lynchie (five men stood up). Worm. DooDoo. DeeDee. Zoonie. Tee. Jughead. Skeeter. Hawkeye. Polly Hawk. Tarbaby. Dickeye. Babe-eye. Mayhog. Bucky Joe. Togun. Lally. Digger. Chet. Higs. Zeke. Spring. Beecho. U-Nuts. Toodie. Reedo. Johnny-O. Chi-Chi. Chickie. Chirpie. Wheels. Westie. Putsy.*"

He made his way around the room and barked out more names as he recognized faces. "*Hollywood. Beaver. Beezer. Snapper. Chico. John-John. RJ. Old Jack. Bulldog. Bubba. Hick. Pieface. Sliver. Deed. Frenchie. KiKi. Kiko. Moose. Ricky Creans. Killer. Snookie. Pepper. Quig. Joey Pompa. Joey I.A. The Bear. Little Jay. Punkie. X. Gusty. Dipper. Happy Dan. Sparrow.*

*Bildo. Hillbilly. Klondike. Geek. Goose. Mad Dog. Keyman. Weird Al. Hugo. Doogo. Jack the Crack. Horace. Soapy. Poochie. Meatball."*

The mayor wasn't spared, *"Pinky!"*

Nor were some of the nuns who taught at Holy Angels, *"Hose Nose. Germ. Mouse. Savage."*

At this point the priests were unable to hide their smiles.

Eddie went on for a good ten minutes longer, picking off as many as he could in the crowd, even inventing some names on the spot for those whom he thought may have felt left out. Finally he circled back to the podium to conclude his remarks.

"You might think I'm just gettin' started. But no, no, I'm near the end. You know I mentioned the tab to you earlier. Well, I want you to remember all the times Eddie let things go when some of you owed me quite a bit of money. I knew you couldn't pay it off at the time for whatever reason. Remember I never charged interest to any of you. Tonight you paid me back in spades. Consider your tickets as the interest that I never charged. And for those of you who didn't pay me back, and a lot of you are here tonight – trust me, *I know who youse are!"*

The crowd roared again and Eddie knew right where to go with it. "You're paying me back now. Tonight. Tonight we take back our school and keep it open for good! But I also want you to know how close-knit a town this is. You just proved it to yourselves. Look at all the people you know by their nicknames. That don't happen in places where people aren't close. And a close community has pride, like this one just proved it has!"

The audience realized the obvious truth of Eddie's statement, a truth that had eluded them for decades, but one that was sitting right in front of them the entire time. All of their collective doubt had been exorcised in one fell swoop when Eddie pointed out that they *could* accomplish big things simply by relying on each other - a spiritual strength that had been living in them all along.

All it took was for an expat from Florida to show up and point it out to them.

# CHAPTER

## 37

The gathering storm had transformed what would have been a balmy mid-June upstate evening into a prematurely darkened landscape. Gusting winds violently shook branches on the dozens of ancient elm trees in the vicinity of Holy Angels.

Rhonda had anticipated it, knowing from experience the havoc early summer storms wrought. Several inches of rain could fall in a few hours and the high winds often left trees uprooted and power lines downed.

She had perhaps 90 minutes of visibility left before she needed to graduate from flashlight to the battery-powered lamp to finish her task. She began in the middle area of the expansive flat roof.

Perusing the first weakened area, she shook her head as she thought back to the inspection report she'd unearthed earlier at the roofing company. The school board had ordered the inspection ten years prior and was made aware of the roof's suboptimal condition, but had elected to forego repairs or replacement because of precarious finances. What were simply worn areas in the capsheet then had progressed to irregular paper-thin defects now, and all it took was O'Rourke's fingernail running along this particular one to create a large rent in the covering.

Running her fingers under the opening, she located the seam that separated the plywood sections, then used a battery-powered screwdriver to back out the screws that held the corner of one of them, enough for her to lift it an inch or two. From the bag she took out a small wooden wedge and inserted it beneath, creating a drain through which the antic-ipated storm water would accomplish her objective.

A little over an hour later, she had created three gaps in the middle of the roof but it was almost totally dark. The wind was increasing even more in velocity. It tossed debris and dust around the rooftop. Some of it found its way into her eyes and she paused several times to clear them. Tablespoon-sized raindrops started to splatter on the roof while jagged bolts of lightning flashed across the sky, each followed by low rumbles of thunder. She knew the window of opportunity was closing - there wasn't much time before the skies opened completely.

Rhonda glanced at her watch – it was almost 10 o'clock. The ban-quet was probably over but she was well aware that people tended to head to the nearby downtown bars afterward.

*Better get this wrapped up before someone finds out what I'm doing,* she thought.

She moved the equipment over to the edge of the roof to begin work on the last spot. She'd need the lamp for this - the flashlight was inadequate without someone to hold it and she needed both hands to work on the seam. Raising the lamp and securing its legs with the weights, she flipped on the switch. She was surprised by the intensity of the beam at first, thinking it too bright and thus more likely to draw attention. But as there was no other option, she resolved to continue on and finish as quickly as possible.

Rain was coming harder now, and the wind picked up even more. As she lifted the corner of the plywood section to insert the wedge she thought he heard the sound of an engine.

Rhonda inched over to the edge of the low wall along the roof's perimeter. At the far entrance of the school parking lot a car was stopped, engine idling, lights on. She started to panic. Could it be the police run-ning a routine security check?

She instinctively flipped the lamp switch off. At that very instant, a gigantic lightning bolt flashed across the sky and illuminated the entire area. She crouched against the perimeter wall, hoping against hope she hadn't been discovered.

*Maybe they'll think it was the lightning they saw up here and not the lamp.*

After a minute or so she peered gingerly over the ledge. The car backed out onto the street, and Rhonda saw the familiar logo of one of the city taxi companies on the side. She breathed a sigh of relief as the taxi sped off.

*Probably someone getting a ride home from the bars downtown, the cabbie's lost or the ride changed their mind.*

She quickly placed the wedge under the plywood, turned off the lamp and packed up the tools. Her work tonight was finished, but she'd return in 24 hours to remove the wedges and screw the seams back together. By then the upper floor of the school would most likely be flooded. No one would discover it until Monday morning, and by then she and Rick would be putting the final touches on a lowball bid for the soon-to-be vacant property.

Before Rhonda closed the rooftop door she paused and looked down at the building where she'd spent three and a half years of her life, the alma mater that never was.

"What goes around, comes around," she muttered.

# CHAPTER

## 38

Several of the board members invited the Wexfords to join them downtown after the banquet to celebrate. They started a pubcrawl at Vito's Bar. From there the group made its way from establishment to establishment, belting out off-key versions of the Holy Angels fight song in between. They were soon joined by O'Toole's posse, which had gotten an earlier start around noon.

By a quarter to ten, Robert looked at his wife through bleary eyes. He knew she had reached her limit, and he wasn't far behind. It was their final night in Westport. Robert had an early flight out of Buffalo the next morning and Ellen managed to obtain the last available seat on the same plane. Robert had checked out of the Hilton Garden earlier in the day and both of them were spending the night at Tilly's. Tilly was also their ride to the airport, and although his tolerance for alcohol was legendary he too was showing plenty of wear and tear by this point in the evening. Robert was concerned enough to call his brother Jimmy and ask him to be ready as a backup in case Tilly wasn't up to it.

The inebriated trio stood at the bar at Lenny O'Leary's and struggled to keep themselves upright. "L-let's get out of here," said Robert, as he balanced his pint glass on the bar.

Tilly let out a massive belch that caught the attention of bystanders. "We ain't driving, my friend. What did Joe Walsh say in the song? Hard to leave the party when you can't find the door, or somethin'."

Ellen was drunk but still had the sense to hail the bartender, who obliged by placing a call for a cab. They would have to return in the morning for their cars before leaving for the airport, but there was no other option.

A few minutes later the revelers stumbled out of the bar into the waiting cab and attempted without success to keep from getting drenched by the steady downpour. Tilly ordered the cabbie to head to his house.

Before they got going Robert reached from the back seat and put his hand on the cabbie's shoulder. "Hey, could you first take us to Holy Angels? I wanna see my old school one last time."

The cabbie shook his head in the affirmative and turned right on the street past the Methodist church tower, then right again at Eddie's store. As they pulled into the high school parking lot, Tilly, riding shot-gun, turned around and discovered the Wexfords both passed out, necks craned backward and mouths agape. He started laughing and then noticed what looked like a bright light coming from the roof of the school.

At that same instant a huge lightning bolt illuminated the entire area, accompanied a split-second later by the loud crack of thunder. Tilly rubbed his eyes and yawned.

*I think I've had too much to drink, I'm seein' things!*

"Hey cabbie, let's go home. My friends are passed out, no sense staying."

By the time they arrived at the house Tilly had passed out as well. The cabbie rousted them awake, collected his fare and disappeared into the driving rainstorm.

# CHAPTER

## 39

The ride to the Buffalo airport the next morning was brutal.

It was good Robert had called Jimmy beforehand. When they arrived at his house in Ganandoqua, Tilly had to run to the bathroom to empty the contents of his stomach. All of them felt the effects of massive hangovers and none were in any condition to drive the car the rest of the way to Buffalo.

And as was his custom whenever he saw his brother in a vulnerable state, Jimmy made a point to needle him relentlessly the entire trip, which was made all the more adventurous by the rainstorm, still in full force. Visibility on the Thruway was poor, which slowed traffic speeds to 30 miles an hour. Nevertheless they made it to their destination in time and the Wexfords made their flight. A few minutes after that Robert and Ellen watched the receding clouds and mist from the comfort of their seats, on their way back to Seattle.

The following Tuesday, Robert was busy at work finishing up a new patient consult when he felt the cell phone vibrating in his back pocket. He pulled it out and saw Ellen's name. Her text read, "Call me ASAP".

He groaned – cryptic messages like this almost always meant bad news.

His assumption was on the money, as Ellen wasted no time getting to the point.

"Rob, you're not going to believe this. I just got off the phone with Ron Alessia. There's a leak in the school roof. The storm over the weekend flooded the upper part of the building. Pretty much all of the classrooms were damaged."

Robert stared at the floor as she spoke. Then he erupted. "What the hell?"

His grip on the phone tightened as Ellen continued. "You know how hard it was raining all Saturday night and Sunday morning. It didn't end until later that day, about five inches altogether. The roofing company said there were places where the covering had worn paper-thin and the rains got through. Not only was there damage to the classrooms but they need a new roof."

Robert asked, "How much is that gonna be?"

"Ron said at least $200,000." She sighed. "But it doesn't end there. It's unbelievable but the school dropped the flood rider on its insurance policy to save money a couple of years ago. They're liable for the inside damage too."

The phone hung loosely from Robert's hand, which dangled at his side. He shook his head back and forth as he breathed heavily.

He heard Ellen's faint voice say something else, so he put the phone back up to his ear. "The school board's meeting tonight. Nothing's been decided but Ron said he doesn't know how they can pay for this. They're probably going to have to close the school after all."

Tears streamed down Robert's face.

# CHAPTER

## 40

To describe the board meeting that Tuesday night as chaotic would have been an understatement. The initial portion was thrown open to the public, and dozens of concerned parents and townspeople filled the room, spilling out into the adjacent hallway.

Father Donovan's opening prayer proved the high mark of its civility. Subsequently, the discourse was peppered with shouting and vituperation. There was an air of desperation as the participants wrestled with the obvious – their school's future was now on life-support.

Millie Flaherty began by raising her arms and pleading for order. "Nothing is going to be accomplished here by shouting and accusations," she said. "The first thing we need is to get the sequence of events from the weekend straight. Ron, could you walk us through what happened?"

Alessia rose from his seat and waited for the din to subside. He cleared his throat and began slowly. "Three of us got here early yesterday morning about 6:30. The first day of summer vacation we have to remove the desks and chairs from the classrooms to strip and wax the floors. When we got up to the second floor we saw water in the hallway and opened the classrooms. Four of them were flooded with about 2 inches. The ceiling tiles were dripping so it was obvious the source was from above. I called Hulse Roofing, and Rhonda came out with a crew and a cherry picker about 10 o'clock. When she came down from the roof she said there were several low areas where the material had worn away and the water had collected and broken through. It looked to her like the damage had been there for some time - the force of the storm was too much for it. She said it had probably been leaking to some minor degree for a while. We didn't notice it until now."

Someone said, "Word is the estimate for replacement is $200,000. Can you verify that?"

Alessia turned his eyes to the crowd. "That's what Rhonda's people are telling us. I have no reason not to believe her. It's a flat roof and the square footage is pretty enormous. Those roofs are harder to replace, more labor- intensive. Most anyone knows the major portion of roof replacement is in the labor."

He looked down and said, "Unfortunately, that's not all we have to contend with. The school dropped the flood coverage rider in our policy a couple of years ago. We were looking for savings and..." He blushed and coughed nervously. "The flood damage is our responsibility now. I'll take the hit for it. The board voted to drop the coverage, but I'm the principal. We didn't have the resources to pay the premium as it was set up. We had no choice but to look for savings. And of course, now the worst case scenario happens."

An uncomfortable silence filled the room, but strangely no one spoke up to criticize. It was as if everyone sensed the futility of engaging in blame at this point. The cost of replacing the roof alone put the probability of the school somehow navigating its way through this latest misfortune at near zero, and they all knew it.

Alessia sensed this and it helped him regain composure. "We also have teachers and administrative staff who need some immediate clarity about job status. Positions at other schools will be filled in a week or so and these folks need to know if they should start looking for other work. Plus there's a whole host of related issues that would need yes or no answers in the next few days. I hate to say it, but we're going to need to decide on the future of Holy Angels pretty much right now. To think that we're going to find another $300,000 or $400,000 or so is, in my opinion, unrealistic. We'd have to have a savior ride in on a horse with that kind of money. And I don't think that's going to happen."

The crowd looked at him in stunned silence as their worst nightmare stared them in the face. One hundred years of Catholic secondary education in Westport was about to come to an inglorious end, just a few days after the community had pulled together in a remarkable show of unity and effort to save it.

A woman in the back of the room was heard quietly sobbing.

The next day the *Westport Times* ran the following headline: Holy Angels To Close. The meeting had indeed resulted in the board voting to cease operations. Around town the mood was glum. The thrill of victory Saturday evening had morphed three short days later into the agony of defeat as yet another foundational pillar was cruelly swept away.

# CHAPTER

## 41

"Gimme a medium pizza with chicken sausage and mushrooms!"

Tilly barked the order to the bartender instead of giving it. He had come to the Villa this Wednesday evening by himself, and he was in a very foul mood. He was consumed by thoughts of all that had happened the past two months – the brainstorming with Robert, the planning, the cajoling of local donors, the trips he and Robert had made to convince Eddie and the out-of-towners to participate. Now everything they had worked for was gone, their dreams shattered.

He stared at his beer, downed it swiftly and ordered another. Tonight he'd take solace in the bottom of a glass.

As he wolfed down the pizza another thought came to him. He knew Robert had been informed of the weekend's disaster but he hadn't personally discussed it with his friend. A glance at his watch told him it was early enough to call. Rob would probably be on his way home from work. He punched the contact number on the cell phone and waited.

"Hey, Tilly - figured you would call pretty soon. I've got you on the Bluetooth in the car. Give me your take on this. Obviously it's a nightmare. But I want to hear what you have to say."

Tilly related his own account of what had transpired at the board meeting. Robert listened carefully as he threaded his way through Seattle commute traffic. He waited for Tilly to pause and then said, "This roofing company - do you know if they were the ones who put it on in the first place?"

Tilly said, "Technically yes and no - let me explain. Hulse *did* install it, I think it was about 40 years ago. That's the life expectancy of a normal roof. But Hulse fell on hard times ten years or so ago. Rhonda bought the company and put it under her little conglomerate."

"Rhonda?" asked Robert.

"Rhonda O'Rourke, of course. Who else has a mini-conglomerate in Westport?" said Tilly. "She turned that operation around. They do good work, actually put my roof on a few years back. Very reliable, good prices."

Robert gazed out at the line of traffic ahead of him as it worked its way over the Lake Washington Bridge. He thought for a moment before his eyes widened a bit as he recalled the conversation with Father Hales at the banquet. Rhonda had been expelled from Holy Angels years before and she had treated him shabbily at their encounter on the downtown street a few weeks ago.

*It would be ridiculous to think.* "Hey, Tilly – just a thought. You know that Rhonda…" He stopped in mid-sentence and reconsidered. *You plant that idea, you better have the facts to back it up. And there aren't any.*

"Oh, never mind."

# CHAPTER

## 42

Father Donovan returned to the rectory after saying the 12:10 Mass at St. Ann's. He sat at the kitchen table, his stomach rumbling. The tuna salad sandwich in front of him looked inviting. He was about to bite into it when the office phone rang. Grabbing the sandwich half, he carried it with him as he made his way down the hall. He bit off a large chunk before picking up the receiver. As a result, his salutation was garbled.

"Hethoo!"

"Hey, Father. Ron Alessia. What are you doing right now?"

The priest struggled to propel the bolus down his esophagus and paused before continuing. "Sorry, Ron. Had pretty much half a sandwich in my mouth. Eating lunch, that's all."

"Stuff the rest of that thing down and hurry over here as soon as you can. I've got some people in my office with important information. You might be interested."

The priest was puzzled. "Why so cryptic? Can't you tell me over the phone? I've got appointments this afternoon starting in 15 minutes."

"Cancel the appointments, Father. Get over here -right now!"

Ten minutes later, the priest stood at the doorstep of Alessia's cramped, windowless office. Tilly sat next to the principal. Facing them were two Hispanic people, a boy and a middle-aged man. As Donovan walked past them he recognized both as Francisco Suarez and his father, Manuel.

"Hello, Ron, Tilly. Hello, Manuel, Francisco," the priest said. He smiled at everyone.

The boy and his father returned the smile and shook the priest's hand. Alessia nodded at Donovan and motioned for him to take a seat. Sensing that something serious was in the air, the cleric sat, still mystified. In truth, he could not possibly have prepared himself for what he was about to hear.

The boy led off with an explanation for the priest. "My father wants to learn English so he can get a better-paying job than the one he has now at the Villa restaurant. For the past six months or so I have been working with him to make that happen. He's made good progress but right now he can understand it better than he can speak it. Actually that's a good and fortunate thing, as you will see."

"Thank God he can understand it!" said Alessia.

"Father, Manuel's already given his story to us in Spanish, and Francisco served as his translator," the principal said. He turned to Francisco and asked, "Perhaps you could go through it in English for Father Donovan in the interest of time? Time is of the essence right now."

Francisco nodded affirmatively and began recounting events for the priest.

"My father's job at the Villa is to wash dishes, help out in the kitchen and make sure the bar is stocked. One evening a few weeks ago he was stacking glasses at the bar. Miss O'Rourke and her boyfriend were sitting there, right near him. They spoke of a plan they had. At the time my father didn't quite understand what they said. They wanted to make sure that Holy Angels closed for good. They hoped it would happen on its own but then the fund drive started. At first they didn't think the fund drive was going to work. But when it looked like it was going to be successful, they had to think of another plan."

Father Donovan said, "Wait a minute. Why did they want the school to close?"

Francisco said, "Mr. Vonderman works for a company that runs trade schools. He and Miss O'Rourke were going to buy the Holy Angels property once it closed and then open a franchise trade school in its place."

Alessia said, "Makes sense, Father. The building doesn't work for purchase unless it's used as a school. There wouldn't have been any interest around here for that. They could have gotten the building and the property for a song after we closed. Remember, there's no trade or vocational school in this area and there's a sufficient number of young high school graduates who would probably enroll if one were available."

The priest frowned and stroked his chin. He said, "And a sufficient number of high school graduates who are ripe for taking out guaranteed student loans to pay the tuition to make the trade school a roaring success and to make big money for Rhonda and Rick."

Alessia pursed his lips as his head moved up and down. He turned to Francisco. "Tell us why your father knows all this."

The boy nodded. "They didn't think he understood English, so they felt comfortable talking in front of him. Miss O'Rourke even said so to Mr. Vonderman. That would have been true maybe a couple of months before, but my father knew enough words and phrases to figure it out right then. Their plan wasn't going to be necessary unless the fund drive worked."

"And what was the plan?" asked the priest.

"Basically, someone was going to poke holes in the roof of the school and then wait for the rains to come. It rained last weekend and the roof leaked after that."

Tilly couldn't contain himself any longer. "Father, when Manuel told us this before you got here, something that happened the night of the banquet popped back into my consciousness. I gotta admit the Wexfords and I drank pretty heavily after the banquet downtown, way too much celebrating. None of us were in any shape to drive. So we called a cab. After we got in, Rob asked the driver to take us past the school. They were leaving the next day and he wanted one last look. Unfortunately both he and Ellen passed out before we got there, and I myself was barely awake. We pulled into the entranceway to the school parking lot and were there for maybe a minute. At first I thought it was a lightning bolt, but I could have sworn I saw a light on the school roof, near the edge, from where we were parked. I had completely forgotten that until hearing this story today.

Maybe someone was up to no good up there? It all fits now that we know this."

Father Donovan had one additional question. "Francisco, this is an amazing story your father tells, but it bothers me from one angle. Why didn't he say anything about it until now? A lot of misery and heartache and expense could have been spared if Manuel had let someone know sooner."

The boy and his father exchanged embarrassed glances. Manuel looked at his inquisitors and said, "Visa!"

Francisco smiled. "My father - you do not understand. It's difficult for anyone from Mexico who is in this country, even legally, to come forward. There is fear of the authorities. Perhaps unjustified fear, as in this case, because my father's papers are in order. I've spoken to him about it. He knows he should have said something earlier. He is ashamed. But he knew he had to come forward now. It was my parents' dream that I graduate from Holy Angels."

The priest rose, walked over and gently put his hand on the man's shoulder. "Don't worry, Manuel. You are very brave, and you've done a great service. We're very proud of you. If what we heard today is corroborated, you'll be regarded as a hero to the people of Westport."

As he spoke the principal picked up the telephone receiver from its cradle and punched numbers on the keypad. After a pause he said solemnly, "May I please speak to the chief of police?"

## 43

Doug Marzetti had served as Westport's police chief for more than 18 years. During that span he thought that he had seen it all. But nothing in his experience was proving as bizarre as what unfolded in front of him right now.

That morning he had taken sworn testimony from Francisco and Manuel Suarez, as well as from a city councilman, Tilly DeAngelo, alleging a plot to sabotage Holy Angels Academy - a plot whose central figures were a prominent local businesswoman and her out-of-town boyfriend.

After consulting with the city attorney and the D.A., he decided it was time to question Rhonda O'Rourke. Marzetti and O'Rourke were acquaintances, and on that basis it was difficult for the chief to believe the allegations being made against her. He felt he owed it to Rhonda to give her a heads-up before driving out for questioning, so he informed O'Rourke of his intentions during a phone call later that morning.

"Oh. Hi, Rhonda. Doug Marzetti here. How's your day going?"

"Hey, Doug. Pretty well. Just hanging around the house out here taking care of some paperwork. Have to go into the office in a couple of hours."

"Oh, good. It sounds like you'd have some time then. Listen, this has to do with the disaster at Holy Angels over the weekend. We're trying to sort out what happened and I've got a few questions for you. Thought maybe you could help us out, seeing as how you're the one who confirmed all the damage up on the roof. A few things aren't adding up and we thought maybe you could help. Can we come out sometime later today to sit down and go through it all?"

"Um, yes. Of course," said Rhonda. Her voice sounded less assured than when she answered the phone. "I, uh, can probably see you around two or so." She paused. "Need to take care of a few things here before then."

"Great," Marzetti said. "I'll be out with the D.A. about two o'clock. Thanks, Rhonda."

Rhonda O'Rourke stared blankly at the antique grandfather clock as she sat on the great room sofa. The "tick-tock" emanating from the family heirloom was the only sound in the entire house. Somehow it was much louder than it ever seemed before.

The only time she'd experienced the same hollow, gut-wrenching feeling that she had now was the day Chemcor filed for bankruptcy.

*There's no way they could have found out! Impossible! I left no trace, there's no evidence. No one knew except Rick and I!*

*Those drunks in the taxi! No, the lightning struck at the exact same instant they could have seen the lamp. They would have called the cops right then, not waited for days to go by. Impossible, but...*

She jumped off the sofa. Any vestige of rational thought was being quickly overwhelmed by an all-consuming panic. She thought back to the nightmarish end of the Chemcor saga. Could history repeat itself? The sinking feeling in her stomach intensified.

The cabinet door in the master bathroom opened slowly. A trembling hand grasped an amber prescription bottle. Moments later, a half dozen pills were parked on a tongue, washed down swiftly with a mouthful of whiskey. Then another half dozen, then another.

At 1:55 pm, Marzetti and the district attorney drove through the entrance to O'Rourke's lakeside estate. The property sloped down to the water, with the house slightly to the left of its center. To the right of and behind the house, they saw a single small craft out in the middle of the lake. The chief paused, momentarily reflecting on the scene's picturesque quality.

Several loud knocks on the front door were met with silence. Finally the attorney tried the door handle, which was unlocked. After opening the door and shouting Rhonda's name - again with no response - they made their way through the great room into the kitchen.

Sitting on the counter was an orange-yellow prescription bottle. It was empty. Marzetti walked over, picked it up and squinted. "Percodan," he said as he glanced back at his counterpart. "Prescription is for 30 tablets."

They searched the entire house but found no sign of its occupant. Next they walked out onto the deck and descended the steps into the back yard. Down at the water's edge was the property's boat dock - minus the boat. Marzetti lumbered across the yard to the neighboring house and banged on the door. A minute later the homeowner opened the door.

"We're looking for your neighbor, Rhonda O'Rourke. Do you happen to know where she could be?"

The man looked bewildered. "Have no idea, sir. I don't know her very well - we're renting for the summer. I've talked to her a couple of times, mainly to get the particulars on our boat operation and things like that."

Marzetti looked toward the boat dock below. "She's got a boat, right? But there's no boat docked down there."

The neighbor agreed. "Yeah, real nice midnight blue speedboat."

The chief's gaze was fixed on an object far out on the lake. "You mean like that one way out there?"

The man squinted in the afternoon sun. "Yes, that looks like it."

Marzetti turned to him and frowned.

"Sir, we need you to give us a ride in that boat of yours, right now!"

# # # # #

Marzetti and the attorney fumbled with their life jackets as the neighbor piloted his boat out onto the lake. As they approached their target a couple of minutes later it was obvious the craft was unoccupied as it tossed and turned in the choppy waves.

"Looks like it's adrift!" shouted the neighbor. "Usually happens when it's not anchored."

After some maneuvering, they finally managed to pull up alongside the boat and steady it. Marzetti carefully planted one, then both feet in the empty craft before rolling over onto its floor, and then balanced himself on hands and knees. In front of him was a note taped to the seat. He sat down and gingerly pulled the paper off. It was a handwritten message, signed by Rhonda O'Rourke. He read it aloud:

"I figured you'd be coming out to arrest me for what happened over the weekend at Holy Angels. You can be assured I did it and that it was my idea alone. Please leave Rick out of this – he wasn't aware of anything. Tell him that I love him and that I'll see him again someday.

As for Chemcor and the way it ended, I know what people think. We did our best to keep the company afloat. Mistakes were made.

I left Westport humiliated once. I'm not up for going through that again."

For what seemed like eternity, the three of them sat silently, waves lapping rhythmically against the boat providing somber accompaniment. Finally the neighbor spoke up. "As I said, there's a reason this boat's so unsteady. I'm looking around and I don't see the anchor. Do you think?"

Marzetti bent over. Below the seat and lying on the floor was a key. "I wonder," he said as he held it up. "Looks like it could be a padlock key. Maybe she tied the anchor around herself and secured two links with the lock. Beforehand, anesthetized herself with a couple dozen Percodans. Waited a while for them to take effect. Then..."

They looked down at the slate-blue water. They knew the chances of finding a body weighed down with a 60-pound anchor in the middle of a lake 600 feet deep were slim and none.

CHAPTER

# 44

In the days that followed, the sensational and bizarre nature of the events in Westport garnered national media coverage. Reporters and camera crews descended on the city, interviewed dozens of locals, dissected the lives of some of the principals involved, even took televised boat rides to the scene of Rhonda O'Rourke's purported demise. One network went so far as to conduct an interview with Ron Alessia on the roof of the school. The story was even featured on Sean Hannity's Fox News television show. Hannity, himself a product of Catholic education, was then instrumental in helping set up a GoFundMe site on the internet where those who wanted to help the school could donate.

Within one week, $750,000 poured in to the site, more than enough for the school to replace its roof and repair the flood damage, with the excess earmarked for a permanent endowment.

The story also resonated with a certain multi-millionaire tech investor in California who happened to be a Holy Angels alumnus. Dennis Richardson, the fellow who had become disillusioned by what he perceived as the school's mismanagement of previous contributions, experienced a change of heart. He called school officials and informed them he'd be open to making a large donation to the permanent endowment contingent on appropriate financial oversight. Informed that this had already been implemented via the recruitment of John Casey, the Chicago accountant, he came through with a $3 million bequest.

Now that those who had interest in sending their children to a Catholic high school had assurances Holy Angels would not only be open for the coming year but also for many years to come, there was a ripple effect on enrollment. The freshman class that August numbered 80, the largest in more than 20 years.

As for the fate of Rhonda O'Rourke, a team of divers was brought in but as expected, efforts proved fruitless. The lake's depth, turbidity, and temperature saw to that, as had proved to be the case for other past searches. A passerby in another craft came forward and described a woman matching O'Rourke's description who was in the boat before she disappeared, but no one actually saw her enter the water. She was presumed drowned by suicide. And the authorities didn't put much stock into her claim in the note that Rick Vonderman was an innocent dupe. They had the eyewitness account of Manuel Suarez to rely on, and Vonderman was charged and subsequently jailed as a flight risk.

# CHAPTER

## 45

Mid-September

Teddy DeLuca gasped for air as the vise-grip on his throat tightened. The defensive tackle's thumbs pressed down on the windpipe and his knees were positioned perfectly across Teddy's shoulders and upper arms to render them useless. Meanwhile another large youngster, an offensive lineman, was similarly positioned across Teddy's ankles.

"Don't you *ever* pull that crap on anyone here again, Teddy!" another voice shouted from the group of half-naked youths circling the boy on the locker room floor. "We don't put up with this stuff here. It may have worked for you at Westport - it won't work at Angels!"

After a few seconds of silence punctuated only by the panting of a dozen or so teenage boys, the tackle slowly relaxed pressure on Teddy's throat, which allowed him to finally draw in air. His face had turned a color somewhere between beet-red and purple, and he had started to lose consciousness. As he rolled over on the wet floor and gradually regained his faculties, he realized that the old act would no longer work in this new environment.

He had gotten himself in the current predicament by cold-cocking a teammate who had soaked Teddy's shower towel in ice water - an Angels team tradition and rite of passage that all freshmen and new-comers were expected to weather without complaint. But this particular newcomer was different. His teammates were well aware of the reputation he had developed as a troublemaker at Westport High – as someone who carried a chip on his shoulder and who spoke with his fists. They had accepted him warily at the start of fall practice and were more than happy to gain his considerable football talent, but he still didn't fit in.

This incident provided the perfect excuse to set him straight.

"Listen, DeLuca," said the big tackle. "All we want you to know is this: you're at our school now, you're on our team and we won't put up with punch-outs over a wet towel. That was supposed to be your initiation. Accept it, OK?"

"OK, OK," replied their victim in a raspy, quavering voice. "I get the point."

The group slowly closed around him and simultaneously extended their hands.

Teddy hesitated and then reluctantly thrust his out as well. He had learned his lesson, and the episode reinforced quite effectively what all of those one-on-one sessions with Coach Herlihy and Mr. DeDomenico hadn't yet accomplished.

*No screwing around with these guys, and no screwing around with this new school.*

# CHAPTER

## 46

Save for the low hum of the overhead fluorescent lights, there was total silence in the cramped office.

The boy sat slumped in his chair, his torso twisted so he faced the single window looking out over the school lawn, doing whatever he could to avoid eye contact with the adults. Behind the desk, Sal DeDomenico narrowed his eyes and shook his head with more than a hint of exasperation.

Meanwhile Dan Herlihy walked over to the boy and placed his huge hands on both shoulders. He spoke in a low, controlled voice. "You know, Teddy, Mr. D has been working with you since late July. He's been very patient. He says he sees signs of progress in your attitude. He likes you personally and thinks you can make it here at Angels. But this latest episode has us both worried. You punched a kid out in the locker room, and that qualifies as assault. The kid could have pressed charges against you. Luckily he doesn't want to, and neither do his parents. They're willing to let it go. But I have to tell you, if something like that happens again, you're out of here. How do you think your mother is going to take that? Do you want to let her down after all she's done and sacrificed to get you in here? You gonna throw that all away by doing something stupid like you did the other day?"

The boy continued to stare out the window. His body faced the two men, but his neck craned awkwardly in the other direction. He did everything in his power to avoid looking their way.

In some way, the pose was a metaphor for his life. It was so much easier to look the other way when things got difficult. At least until the fits of spasmodic, uncontrollable rage that too-often marked his behavior erupted.

Bam!

His fist came out of nowhere and slammed into the desktop with frightening force. "Dammit! Dammit!" he screamed at the top of his lungs. "What is wrong with me? Why am I so pissed off? I hate myself!"

As the boy snapped his head around and shouted, his eyes narrowed and the mop of hair on his head slapped the side of his face. He looked directly at DeDomenico.

The counselor saw the two tiny brown eyes and a chill instantly went up his spine. He'd seen that look only once before.

*On a dark street long ago.*

He sat there, frozen. The coach took notice. "You OK, Sal?"

"Oh! Uh......yeah. Lost my train of thought, coach."

He dabbed the corner of his mouth and wiped his nose. It required every ounce of composure he could muster to continue the conversation. He cleared his throat. "Teddy, you know me by now, you know I'm your friend. You know you can trust me - you can trust coach. You've made tremendous progress since we started in July. Once school started you made good on your promise to work as hard as you could in class. You have pretty good grades, the teachers like you, you've made some friends. And you've been everything advertised on the football field - leading the conference in rushing, 14 touchdowns. We're undefeated and in first place. You've got the school and the town eating out of your hand, but you can't beat kids up who pull an innocent prank on you. Don't you see? That was a rite of passage. Those boys want to accept you - all you had to do was laugh it off and do it yourself to the next unsuspecting kid. That's the tradition.

"No one is trying to single you out - it's not like before. Look, you're angry and you know why? I think it's because your father isn't in your life. We feel for you. It isn't easy growing up without a father, but you've got to accept that and make the best of it. Turn lemons into lemonade. You've got father figures here - me, coach. There are plenty of us who care about you and who are willing to help fill that void. Now, you can make excuses for yourself and go down the path your were on at Westport, or you can make a new path - you choose. But if you go the old way, I can guarantee you won't be doing it here at Holy Angels. You'll be out of here before you know it. Understand?"

The boy sobbed uncontrollably, but nodded in assent.

Both of the adults felt like joining him.

Especially the one sitting behind the desk.

# CHAPTER

## 47

Mary DeLuca finished checking in the hotel guests at Westport-On-The-Lake and then hopped in her car. She had made it a point to pick up her son from school after every football practice, purposely leaving him no option after that but homework and supper. It was by design, on the advice of Sal DeDomenico and the football coaches - a coordinated effort to keep Teddy on the straight and narrow.

And so far, with the one exception of the locker room incident, it seemed to be working. Teddy was noticeably happier and more positive. He'd been a big shot at Westport High the previous year but only because of his gridiron exploits. Now he was gaining respect, not only for football but also for his effort in the classroom.

Before he was a badass. He was slowly but surely shedding that label at Holy Angels.

As his mother sat in the car and waited for Teddy to emerge from the side door of school, she saw a figure in the side mirror approaching from behind. A familiar figure it was - tilted to one side, leaning on a cane. She turned her head to greet Sal.

"Hey there, counselor. How's it going?"

She smiled as he carefully made his way onto the strip of lawn separating the sidewalk from the curb.

"Hi, Mary. Very well. Can I speak with you for a moment? Do you mind if I sit in your car? It's hard..."

"Of course. Come around," she said as she leaned over to open the passenger door.

He limped around and climbed in, then leaned his head back and exhaled slowly.

"Wanted to bring you up to date on Teddy. He seems to be doing well since the locker room thing. I think the talk Dan and I had with him was therapeutic. Some things got out there that we discussed - things that in the long run I think will be good for him."

"Like what?" she asked, with a look of concern.

"Well..." He paused and stared straight ahead.

"Come on, Sal. Say it. What kind of things?"

He pivoted sharply toward her. In the most serious tone he could muster, he looked her in the eye and said, "Mary, who is Teddy's father?"

She stared at him for a few seconds. Her eyes glazed over and she looked out the windshield. She swallowed hard and began in a flat cadence. "You know who his father is. I figured it was only a matter of time before it hit you. Oh, God, the irony."

Her voice quivered as she continued. "Danny left me as soon as he found out I was pregnant. We tracked him down and got him to acknowledge he was the father but he never had contact with Teddy after he was born. Oh, he'd pay child support for a while and then move to a different address or town. They'd track him down, he'd pay a little more, then move again. Finally he disappeared. I don't know where he is now. But when we were together, when he was very drunk one night, he told me about the attack on Oak Street. He was remorseful but not to the point where he would have talked to you about it."

"He was a coward. Not just for that, but for what he did to Teddy."

She turned to her visitor, still fighting back tears. "Salvatore DeDomenico, you are the finest human being I've ever known. What you and the others..." She gestured at the school. "And this place. What you are doing for my son is beyond anything I could have dreamed of. For the first time, I'm seeing direction and purpose in him. He's becoming what I had hoped beyond hope he could be. I will always be grateful to you, especially knowing that you - you've basically extended a hand to the son of the man who almost killed you."

Sal reached across the seat, looked down and grasped her hand tightly. There was nothing more he could say.

# CHAPTER

## 48

*Early October*

A picture-perfect full harvest moon hung high above Northside Stadium. Below, the crowds filed past the entrance gates in anticipation of the most important football game in recent memory for Holy Angels Academy.

It was homecoming and on this warm early fall Friday night the visiting Wellington Indians hoped to crash the party, upset the home team and claim the Western Division regular-season title. The only blemish on their record was a close loss to a Ganandoqua squad earlier in the season that benefited from an early-game injury to the Wellington quarterback.

The winner of tonight's game would gain a berth in the conference title matchup the following weekend against the Eastern Division champion Westport Panthers. The Angels were undefeated and determined to put away Wellington, thereby setting up a titanic battle with their cross-town rivals.

The game had additional meaning for Holy Angels. After all, the school wasn't even supposed to be open now, but the magical fund drive and the strange events of early summer had changed all that. And the $3 million gift from Dennis Richardson had put to rest any doubts people had about the school's future.

Some of the folks intimately involved in those events were in attendance tonight. Robert Wexford had flown in from Seattle, joined by his childhood friend and fellow paperboy, John Patterson. Father Hales had driven down from Rochester. The three of them met up on the Angels sideline with Tilly DeAngelo, Ron Alessia and Sal DeDomenico.

From the start the game was a hard-hitting, seesaw contest.

Wellington drew first blood as they used a precision West Coast passing attack to move down the field after taking the opening kickoff, a 20-yard slant pass over the middle resulting in an early 7-0 lead.

Holy Angels answered in the second quarter with a methodical drive powered by their all-conference running back, Teddy DeLuca. He carried on eight of the 11 plays, eventually plowing in for the touchdown from two yards out. That brought the Angels within one, but the extra point failed.

A defensive struggle ensued with neither team able to mount any serious drive until late in the third quarter, when the Indians used a series of short passes and runs, punctuated by another crossing route, to extend their lead. Another missed extra point resulted in a score of 13-6, Wellington. Holy Angels again got their ground game going early in the fourth quarter, marching down to the Wellington 17 where they failed to convert on third-and-two. The resulting field goal left them on the short end of a 13-9 score.

With less than two minutes left in the game, Wellington had a fourth-and-one on the Angels 29-yard line. A first down would have allowed them to run out the clock for the victory. But during an ensuing timeout the Angels coaching staff had guessed correctly the play call would be a run to the right, instructing the defense to shift to that side before the snap.

No gain – Angels ball!

With only one timeout of their own remaining and the clock running, the home side was 71 yards away from the go-ahead and likely winning touchdown. A screen pass, a sideline completion, and a surprise quarterback sneak up the middle had them just across midfield with 42 seconds left on the clock.

Coach Dan Herlihy motioned for the final timeout. With his squad gathered around him on the sideline, he noted that many of them stood with their hands on hips and gasped for breath - a reliable sign the team was about out of gas. He knew it was time to go for broke, so he instructed them to run the play they had considered their ace in the hole, the one they had saved for just such an occasion.

"OK guys, listen up! Listen up! Ricky Z Flat 32! Ricky Z Flat 32! Now get out there and kick butt! Win it!"

As the team broke the huddle, Teddy DeLuca ran to his assigned position in the slot on the right side of the formation. But instead of concentrating on his assignment, he was inexplicably haunted by a momentary flashback to events of earlier in his life. Growing up in Florida, moving from apartment to apartment with his mother, the poverty, the fistfights and school suspensions, the anger, the depression, the father he never had – all of it running through his head in the space of a second or two.

His trance was interrupted by the quarterback's cadence. Teddy tilted his head slightly left to look for the center snap, and when it happened he took two steps to the right, then turned 180 degrees and ran as fast as he could across the field to the left flat. Meanwhile the quarterback faked a handoff to the fullback and ran into the right flat, the area Teddy had just vacated.

All eyes were now on the quarterback as the defense anticipated a pass or a keeper around right end. However, DeLuca was now all alone in the left flat. With Wellington defenders bearing down on him, the quarterback kept his eyes directly downfield until the last possible moment, then pivoted and lofted an arcing pass to his teammate, who was still the only player on the other side of the field.

Teddy reeled in the looping toss and surveyed the landscape. One of the Wellington linebackers, although initially duped by the play's misdirection, had recovered and closed in on him from the right. As the defender drew near, Teddy looked right and then planted his left foot toward the sideline. The linebacker reached for it only to sprawl awkwardly on his belly as Teddy deftly withdrew it, angled diagonally right and headed upfield.

The crowd was on its feet roaring, and the roar increased exponentially as DeLuca broke into the clear following the masterful fake. He was now into the second level, angling across the field toward the end zone.

And with his speed, no one was going to catch him. The boundary-side cornerback came up from behind, but Teddy had a step on him and the angle. All he had to do was keep running and - game over!

But then a strange thing happened on the road to certain victory. The roar of the crowd dialed back somewhat as people looked on in disbelief at what was transpiring. Teddy's momentum slowed, and he looked around to his pursuit.

*It was as though he wanted the defender to catch up to him!*

And catch up he did. When that happened Teddy turned and accelerated, driving his shoulder into the cornerback's midsection and sending him flying backward, landing with a sickening thud.

A tremendous roar went up again from the crowd. Teddy resumed his full-tilt sprint to the end zone.

At that instant on the Holy Angels sideline, Robert Wexford and his friends looked around in unison at the man behind them, the man leaning on his cane.

Sal DeDomenico slowly shook his head, and smiled.